How to Make a Wedding

Eloise Evans is an in-demand luxury bridal designer from Sydney.

Victoria Preston is a talented wedding cake creator from Boston.

Worlds apart, they should have only their industry in common, but they also share an unexpected bond—they're long-lost twin sisters!

Now, as their worlds collide, Eloise and Tori find the pieces of themselves they've always felt have been missing...just in time for each of them to find the love they deserve...

Read the twin sisters' stories in

From Bridal Designer to Bride
By Kandy Shepherd

From Tropical Fling to Forever
By Nina Singh

D1359009

Dear Reader,

Are you, like me, fascinated by identical twins? I particularly love stories about twins separated as babies and reunited as adults. So you can imagine the fun I had writing *From Bridal Designer to Bride*.

Boston billionaire Josh Taylor gets involved in the search for Eloise Evans, the long-lost twin sister of his friend Tori. He doesn't expect to fall in love with quirky bridal designer Eloise—or to get tangled up in her world of weddings, bridezillas and rescue dogs.

Eloise has always felt she's been missing something in her life. Turns out it's not only her twin but also a man like Josh. These two are made for each other—but there are issues in both their pasts they have to work through before they can open their hearts to that once-in-a-lifetime love. I hope you enjoy reading how Eloise and Josh find their own happy-ever-after.

Eloise's story is the first of the duet How to Make a Wedding. Watch out for the story of her twin, Tori, *From Tropical Fling to Forever* by Nina Singh, next month.

Warm regards,

Kandy

From Bridal Designer to Bride

Kandy Shepherd

Recycling programs
for this product may
not exist in your area.

ISBN-13: 978-1-335-56695-9

From Bridal Designer to Bride

Copyright © 2021 by Kandy Shepherd

This edition published by arrangement with Harlequin Books S.A.

For questions and comments about the quality of this book, please contact us at CustomerService@Harlequin.com.

Harlequin Enterprises ULC
22 Adelaide St. West, 40th Floor
Toronto, Ontario M5H 4E3, Canada
www.Harlequin.com

Printed in U.S.A.

Kandy Shepherd swapped a career as a magazine editor for a life writing romance. She lives on a small farm in the Blue Mountains near Sydney, Australia, with her husband, daughter and lots of pets. She believes in love at first sight and real-life romance—they worked for her! Kandy loves to hear from her readers. Visit her at kandyshepherd.com.

Books by Kandy Shepherd

Harlequin Romance

Christmas at the Harrington Park Hotel

Their Royal Baby Gift

Sydney Brides

Gift-Wrapped in Her Wedding Dress
Crown Prince's Chosen Bride
The Bridesmaid's Baby Bump

A Diamond in Her Stocking
From Paradise...to Pregnant!
Hired by the Brooding Billionaire
Greek Tycoon's Mistletoe Proposal
Conveniently Wed to the Greek
Stranded with Her Greek Tycoon
Best Man and the Runaway Bride
Second Chance with the Single Dad
Falling for the Secret Princess
One Night with Her Millionaire Boss

Visit the Author Profile page
at Harlequin.com for more titles.

In memory of my wonderful long-time friend, Jan Herbert, taken recently by ovarian cancer. Jan enjoyed my books and had her own real-life romance in a long and very happy marriage to Ric. When she became unable to read, he read my stories to her. "Your books gave her pleasure and that was a wonderful gift," he told me. *Vale,* Jan, you are so missed.

Praise for
Kandy Shepherd

PROLOGUE

JOSH TAYLOR WATCHED the expressions of disbelief and amazement flash across his friend Tori Preston's face as she scrutinised the images of the woman in the glossy magazine.

'Can you see the resemblance?' Josh asked.

Tori continued to stare at the image of the beautiful blue-eyed woman with the dark hair that tumbled around her shoulders. His friend looked back up at Josh, a frown pleating her forehead. 'Except that my hair is cut so short and we have a different way of dressing we... we're identical. How can this be?'

'Immediately I thought she must be related to you. A cousin maybe. Out of curiosity I looked her up,' Josh said. 'She's an Australian fashion designer named Eloise Evans.'

He wasn't going to admit it to Tori but, while he had only ever seen Tori as a strictly platonic friend, there was something about Eloise Evans that fascinated him. He'd read through the article about her several times as he debated whether or not he should point out the uncanny resemblance to Tori.

'Not only is she twenty-eight, like you, but she also has the same birthdate.'

Tori paled. 'You're kidding me?'

Josh shook his head. 'There's more. While she lives in Sydney, Australia now, she was born here in Boston. In this interview, she makes no secret of the fact she was adopted as a two-year-old toddler.'

Tori drew a sharp intake of breath. She looked up at Josh, her cornflower-blue eyes troubled. 'I've always known I was adopted when I was two years old, after my birth mother died.'

'I know,' he said.

She peered harder at the image on the page, the woman smiling a smile so very like Tori's own. 'You know, I feel I've seen her before.'

Josh laughed. 'Seems you might see her every time you look in the mirror.'

Tori shook her head. 'It's not that. My memory of someone like this is of a little girl. My imaginary friend, my mum used to call her, when I spoke about her. But I stubbornly insisted she was real.'

'It could all be a coincidence,' said Josh, knowing it seemed like one coincidence too many.

Tori looked up at him. 'What if it isn't? What if...what if there were two babies?'

Josh paused. 'Adopted to different families, you mean?'

'Twins,' Tori said.

'Twins?' he echoed.

'I need to meet her, see if there could be any truth in this. Oh, my goodness, Josh, what if...? But Australia. It's so far away and it's such a busy time for me at work with the spring wedding season in full swing.' Tori was the wedding cake baker of choice to the elite of Boston.

Josh paused. 'Why don't you let me scout her out first? I have to visit Australia for business next week. Why don't I look this Eloise Evans up for you?'

Tori's eyes widened. 'You'd do that?'

Tori and her brothers had been so supportive of him when his own sibling had disowned him. He could never repay her enough for her friendship. 'Of course. In the meantime, why don't you talk to your parents and

see if they know anything about the circum-
stances of your adoption? This could be a
crazy coincidence, or…'

'Or… I might have a twin sister,' Tori
breathed.

CHAPTER ONE

JOSH TAYLOR WAS a highly successful entrepreneur; a billionaire at age twenty-nine. He possessed multiple effective business skills, but it seemed engineering a face-to-face meeting with his friend Tori's possible twin sister, Eloise Evans, wasn't one of them.

Tori had discovered there had indeed been twin baby girls put up for adoption, and there was a very good chance the Australian woman was her birth sister. 'Just get close enough so you can see for yourself if she really does look just like me in real life,' Tori had asked.

Within a day of arriving in Sydney, Josh had tracked down Eloise Evans. He'd learned that her high-end bridal wear business was considered among the best in the country and had a growing international reputation. He had scoped out her elegant Eloise Evans

Atelier headquarters in the exclusive inner eastern suburb of Double Bay in the hope of catching sight of her. But days later he still had not seen even a glimpse of the elusive bridal designer.

On Saturday morning, his last day in Sydney, he'd switched track and was looking out for her near her apartment in Rushcutters Bay. The nineteen-thirties-style apartment building faced a park and he sat in the balmy autumn sunshine on a bench near the low sandstone sea wall that separated the park from the sparkling blue waters of Sydney Harbour.

His seat was carefully chosen for the unimpeded view of Eloise's building, but still there was no sight of her. He bent his head to text Tori the news that unfortunately he hadn't been able to make contact.

But then something made him look up. A peal of feminine laughter. The barking of an excited dog. And there she was. Eloise Evans emerged from the shade of the large trees that formed the perimeter of the park. She had a dog on a lead and was heading across the park towards the water—and him. He recognised Eloise instantly, even from this distance, this woman who'd grabbed his attention on the pages of that magazine. There could be no doubt she was Tori's doppelganger.

As she crossed the grass and came closer, Josh got up from the park bench and started to head towards her. Thoughts of how to engineer an 'accidental' meeting pushed insistently through his mind. Tori might think it a good idea to bump into Eloise but he realised it was a very bad idea. She would take him for, at best, a mugger, at worst, a groper. It would be better to stroll by and take a quick sideways glance at her face to confirm, and then continue on his way.

As she and her dog got closer his heart started to thud and his mouth went dry. It was uncanny. Not only was there a remarkable facial similarity but the Australian designer was also the same height, around five feet seven, and had the same slim build as his friend Tori. They *must* be related.

But the more he looked, the more he noticed the differences rather than the similarities. Ms Evans seemed to waft rather than walk along the pathway, whereas Tori would stride. Her black hair fell to her shoulders in a thick, glossy mass—the opposite of Tori's spikey crop. When Tori walked her dogs, she wore jeans or gym pants. Eloise Evans was dressed in a narrow calf-length skirt made of some kind of lacy fabric in a rich cinnamon colour with a cream top that was tied to show off her narrow waist and high, round breasts. To tell the truth, he had scarcely ever noticed Tori's curves—she was more like the sister he'd never had than a girl whose figure he noticed in any way other than the abstract.

As Eloise Evans walked, the skirt split to reveal tantalising glimpses of long, slender legs, and he noticed them—*man, did he notice*. Josh took a short, sharp breath. That was the main difference between this woman and his friend back home in Boston—he found this woman *hot* in an ultra-feminine, sensual way. He didn't want to get caught ogling her but it was difficult not to stare—she was utterly gorgeous.

As she got closer she veered away, heading for the nearby off-lead dog play area, by the look of the bright yellow dog ball launcher she carried. He should leave it at that.

But he had made a deal with Tori that he would observe her possible sister as closely as he could. He'd also promised, if he actually made contact with her, that he would not say anything about Tori.

And when Josh gave his word he did his

best to honour it. He had spent his first sixteen years living his mother's lie—turned out
the man he'd thought his father wasn't his father at all. The discovery of her secret, and his
subsequent abandonment by his family, had
seared a hatred of lies and dishonesty onto
his soul. He didn't give or take trust easily.

Eloise Evans's dog was somewhat at odds
with her glamorous appearance. Pure mutt,
by the look of it. Small, with a mess of black,
ginger and white fur. Josh took note, as he
knew Tori would want to know all about
the dog. As it neared the dog park the mutt
started to prance with excitement, pulling at
its lead, and yapping.

'Okay, okay,' Ms Evans said, laughing as
she bent down to unfasten the lead from its
harness. Josh froze. Her laugh. It was like
Tori's but not like Tori's. This woman's laugh
was low, musical and immediately he wanted
to hear it again. She ruffled the fur around
the dog's neck in a casual caress. *That lucky,
lucky dog.*

Now she was dangerously close. Close
enough to affirm there was a very good
chance this woman could be Tori's twin. His
time here was done. He'd got what he came
for. Mission accomplished. He should walk

away in the opposite direction. And yet he lingered, taking slow steps, unable to take his eyes off the beautiful woman who only had eyes for her dog.

Eloise Evans launched a green tennis ball and the little dog took off, grabbed it in its mouth, scampered back to her and proudly dropped the ball at her feet. 'Good girl, Daisy,' she crooned, her voice husky and sweet and warm with affection.

Josh paused to savour the sound of her voice. It reminded him of a time before he'd locked up his heart against hurt and betrayal. She scooped up the ball and launched it again. The dog rushed to catch it, but this time the ball bounced off its nose and shot towards the water—and Josh. Instinctively he reached up and caught it—smack—hard in his hand.

He was about to throw it back when Eloise Evans hurried up to him, the dog at her heels. 'Well caught. Thank you.'

Josh shrugged with feigned nonchalance to cover his shock at her sudden close proximity. He caught a tantalising drift of her sweet, floral scent. 'An easy catch.' When he was twelve years old he had dreamed of playing baseball for Boston's Red Sox. All the practice had paid off today.

'Seriously, that's her favourite ball. She'd have tried to swim after it if it had gone into the water. And then we'd be in trouble.' Her accent was Australian, while Tori's was pure Boston. But the voice was uncannily similar.

This close, Josh could tell Eloise had the same blue eyes as Tori, the same full, curving mouth, the same small, straight nose. Like Tori's, her beauty wasn't one of vapid prettiness. There was strength in the set of her chin, intelligence in the intensity of her gaze. He could readily believe they were identical twins. But she was also very different from Tori in ways too subtle for him to articulate. More of a feeling than anything substantial. There was something about her he found extraordinarily appealing—had done so from when he'd first spotted her image in that magazine. In real life the impact of her presence knocked the breath out of him. But, lovely as he found her, Ms Evans could only be the subject of his investigation on behalf of his friend.

He forced his voice to sound normal. 'You're so welcome,' he said. 'Glad to be of help.'

He knew he should hand the ball over immediately. But the longer he held on to it, the longer he had the opportunity to enjoy being closer to Eloise Evans. Unexpectedly, the little dog ran up and stood up straight to put both front paws on Josh's knees. She looked up at him with gentle brown eyes, pink tongue lolling, and he swore she was smiling.

'Hi there,' he said, bemused when the dog made no move to remove her paws. She wagged her plumed tail in response.

'Daisy!' Eloise admonished.

'She's okay,' he said. 'I guess she wants her ball back.'

'Thank you for not objecting to her jumping up on you. I've never seen her do anything like that before. She's usually scared of men. It's awesome she trusts you.'

Josh looked down into the little dog's sweet face. He wanted to reach down and stroke her but didn't want to risk frightening her.

'Did someone hurt her?'

'Undoubtedly. She was found dumped on the side of a busy road. Just skin and bone, an injured leg. No ID, no microchip. Just abandoned when someone tired of her.' Eloise's voice hitched. 'Thankfully a good person from a dog rescue centre was able to catch her.'

Josh swore under his breath. 'Surely there's

a special place in hell reserved for people who hurt animals.'

'I certainly hope so,' she said vehemently.

'So you adopted her?'

She shook her head. The sun picked up blueish glints in her black hair. The kind of thick, luxuriant hair he would like to run his fingers through. Not that he'd ever get the chance with lovely Eloise Evans. Not when his promise to Tori stood in the way. Not when Eloise lived on the other side of the world. Especially not when he had goals to achieve by the time he reached thirty that didn't allow for distraction.

'I love dogs but I can't have one full-time right now,' she said. 'I have to travel for work too often and…'

She stopped, perhaps aware she'd revealed too much to a stranger. The rest of her words came out in a rush. 'So I foster rescue dogs and keep them with me until they're ready to go to a forever home.'

Just like Tori did. Tori was passionate about dog rescue, and they both worked in the wedding business. The similarities between them were more than skin deep. The thought crossed his mind that if the two women ever met they'd find a lot in common.

'It's great Daisy is safe with you,' he said. 'She seems a very nice dog.'

'She's a sweetheart. When I first got her she would cower with her tail between her legs if she ever got near to a man. For her to have taken to you is a huge step forward.'

If it were Tori, Josh would joke it was purely because of his natural charisma and she would slap him down in a sisterly manner. Instead with Eloise he was serious. 'I'm glad to hear that,' he said. 'Shall I throw her ball for her?'

'Oh, my gosh, you've still got it in your hand. Is it horrible? I mean, covered in doggy slobber?' She looked at him, and he could tell she was trying not to laugh at his dilemma. *She was enchanting.*

'It is a tad on the damp side, but what do you expect from a well-loved dog ball?' He didn't think wiping his hand down the side of his trousers in disgust was the way to impress Ms Evans.

'I'm glad you understand.' Her lips curved into a smile that lit her blue eyes. 'I'm sure Daisy would love you to throw her ball for her.'

Josh had grown up with dogs. He donated substantial sums to dog rescue organisations. But he didn't want the responsibility of owning one himself. He never wanted to be tied down by anything or anyone. Not even a dog. Certainly not a woman. He'd been driven to prove himself to people who didn't believe in him and that had left no room for emotional entanglements that might have hindered his race for his first million, then the next and the next.

Eloise handed him the launcher. He looked down at Daisy. 'Do you want your ball?' The dog yapped her assent, her eyes following the ball. Josh was determined to throw it as far and fast as he could. For the dog's enjoyment, of course. Not just to impress Eloise with a testosterone-fuelled show of strength.

The ball flew across the width of the park and Daisy scampered after it. 'She's loving it,' said Eloise, clapping her hands in enthusiasm. 'I could never throw the ball that far.'

The little dog ran back, ball triumphantly in her mouth. She paused, her eyes going from Josh to her foster mother. Then she deposited it at Josh's feet, sat and looked up at him. He felt curiously moved by the gesture. Eloise's eyes were misty and her voice unsteady. 'That's really something. Thank you. I never thought she'd trust a man with her precious ball.'

He had to clear his throat. 'Shall I throw it again?'

'Please,' she said.

Josh threw the ball and again the little dog brought it back to him. Only this time she came back via the muddy area around the doggy watering station. Her paws were dark with mud, and before Josh could stop her she jumped up and streaked mud on his biscuit-coloured linen trousers.

'Daisy! No!' Eloise took hold of her dog's harness and gently tugged her down. 'I'm sorry. She didn't mean to make that mess,' she said to Josh.

'Of course she didn't,' he said. He patted Daisy to show there were no hard feelings. She smiled her doggy smile.

'I hope she hasn't ruined your trousers.' Eloise had a small handbag crossed over her shoulder. She burrowed into it and pulled out a handful of tissues. 'Take these. They're clean. Might get the worst off. You can't use a wet cloth on mud; water makes it worse.'

He took the tissues and wiped the surface dirt off his trousers. 'It's okay,' he said. 'It's just mud.'

'I know about fabrics. That's very good linen. Mud can stain. Of course, I'll pay for your trousers to be dry cleaned. Or replaced if you can't get the stain out.'

'There's no need. Really. I have other trousers.' He'd have them dry cleaned at the hotel. If the mud stained, he'd throw them out. It would be worth it for the story he'd tell Tori. She loved a good dog story.

'I insist.'

'I refuse.'

'So we've reached an impasse,' she said, a smile tugging at the corners of her mouth.

'It appears so,' he said.

'Can I at least buy you a coffee? Daisy and I usually go for coffee at a dog-friendly café further up in the park and we're heading that way now. Would you like to join us?'

Josh didn't hesitate. The dog had decided this course of action and this was a better way to make contact with Eloise than he could ever have engineered himself. *Thank you, Daisy.*

'I'd like that very much,' he said.

CHAPTER TWO

ELOISE WOULD NORMALLY never invite a man she'd just met in the park for a coffee. The words had just slipped out of her mouth, much to her own astonishment. However, strictly speaking, it was Daisy who had made the approach. Eloise could still hardly believe the little dog had displayed such trust in the tall American when she was normally so wary of men. It was a huge step forward in her rehabilitation. *Dogs could be very good judges of character.*

She looked up at the man. With his thick brown hair, lean face and hazel eyes he was strikingly handsome. Probably around her age, she figured. He'd been so kind to Daisy, a little survivor who was in such need of kindness. And he'd been so good about the mud on his very expensive-looking trousers when he was quite within his rights to be cranky. The least she could do was offer him a coffee. He was a stranger and she should be cautious but there was actually very little risk to her in doing so—she was a regular at the café and she could always find a table out in the open for Daisy or the other dogs she had fostered.

'I'm glad you can join us. However, if you change your mind about letting me pay for your dry cleaning just say so.'

'I won't change my mind and I'm looking forward to the coffee. I'm Josh Taylor, by the way.'

'Eloise Evans,' she said. 'And you've met Daisy, of course. Let me put her lead back on. The café is further down the park.'

They started to stroll along the waterfront path towards the café. She never tired of the sight of myriad yachts moored near the yacht club, the distant view of the Sydney Harbour Bridge. This was one of the most elite areas of the city.

Eloise appreciated the way Josh Taylor slowed his long stride to accommodate Daisy trotting happily along between them. This was a man who genuinely liked dogs.

'You're American. Do you live here? Or are you visiting Sydney?'

'I'm visiting for a few days.'

'Business or pleasure?' she asked.

'A business trip,' he said. 'Although it's always a pleasure to visit Australia.'

'Let me guess,' she said. 'You're from Boston.'

'Correct,' he said. 'I'm told we have a distinctive accent, although I don't hear it myself, of course.'

'My dad was from Boston,' she said. 'Your accent is like his. It's nice to hear it again. Brings back happy memories.'

'Was?'

'He died thirteen years ago when I was fifteen. I adored him and still miss him.'

'I'm sorry,' he said.

She made a dismissive gesture. 'It was a long time ago.' She didn't want a gloomy conversation, although her heart still spasmed with grief every time she thought about her father.

At the café, she and Josh were quickly shown to her favourite table outside, in the shade of an awning and near to the doggy water bowl. She noticed the little dog's tail went down at the friendly male waiter's greeting but wagged when Josh showed her attention. 'You've certainly won her heart,' she said.

He grinned. 'Could be my magnetic personality, but she can probably sense I like dogs. My dog was my best friend when I was a kid. Sadly, I travel a lot and—like you—I'm not in a position to have my own dog right now.'

Daisy had taken a shine to Josh Taylor and Eloise found herself drawn to him too. In her experience it wasn't often you got both outrageously handsome and personable in one man. These were only first impressions of course, and she couldn't always trust them. But she could trust her dog's instincts. 'It gives me hope we can get her over her nervousness with men. Though she'll probably do better rehomed with a woman.'

Josh looked into her face and she saw compassion in his hazel eyes. 'It must be hard to let a foster dog go when you've put so much care into them.'

'I fall in love with them every time. Saying goodbye is hard. But I have to force myself not to get too attached. The work I put into them helps them get a forever home, then frees me up to socialise another traumatised dog. Most of the dogs' new owners keep in touch and send me photos.' She reached down to pet Daisy, who sat between them.

'She's a lucky little dog to be cared for so well by a kind person like you.'

Eloise surprised herself by blushing. 'Thank you.'

Their coffees arrived. An espresso for him, a cappuccino for her, and a 'puppuccino' for Daisy, served in a shot-sized paper cup. 'It's just frothed lactose-free milk, no harmful chocolate or caffeine,' she explained.

'What's life without an occasional treat?' Josh said, smiling.

'I like your philosophy,' she said with an answering smile.

She liked *him*. It was a long time since she'd felt so at ease in a man's company. He was easy to chat to and she had no trouble opening up to strangers. It was one of the reasons her business did so well. Apart from the superb design, craftsmanship and sheer beauty of her couture wedding gowns, her clients also had a warm, friendly shopping experience. Eloise had a gift for drawing them out, particularly the shy brides, and to do that she had to sometimes share some of her own life.

'You must be enjoying the glorious weather we're having here,' she said. 'I imagine it's getting chilly back in Boston now.' Weather was always a safe topic for conversation.

'Mild one day and back to winter the next. That's typical. You said your dad came from Boston. Have you visited there?'

'I was actually born in Boston,' she said.

'Really?' he said.

'I left there when I was eight years old.'

'So you're an Aussie now?'

'I have dual citizenship. My mother is Australian and my father was American.'

'Best of both worlds,' he said.

'I think of it that way.'

'What brought your family back here?'

'My dad used to joke it was the relatively mild winters we have in Sydney.'

'I can see the appeal,' he said. 'Boston winters are bitterly cold.'

'I remember.' She pretended to shiver and wrapped her arms around herself, which made him smile. 'But seriously, my mother got homesick. Her family was here. When he was alive we used to go "home" to Boston to visit my grandparents.'

She didn't want to tell him that conflicting loyalties between Australia and the United States had put stresses on their family. Her grandparents had never forgiven her mother for taking her father away and she'd lost touch with them after he'd died. That was only part of it, though. The more painful truth was that they didn't consider her their 'real' grandchild. Not when she was adopted and not her father's 'real' child. Not that her father had thought that. Not at all. *'My darling daughter,'* he'd used to call her. DD for short.

Which had made it all the more painful when she'd discovered, quite by accident, at age thirteen, that she was adopted. She'd needed a vaccination certificate for school and had burrowed through where she knew her parents kept the family medical records. And there it was, proof she'd been born to a Boston woman who had died when Eloise was two, and then adopted to the people she'd believed she'd been born to. There was a notation on the document that the family history of both parents was unknown.

She'd been too stricken by shock to move. Just stood there with the document in her hand for heaven knew how long. How hurt and angry she'd been, how betrayed she'd felt, how humiliated that everyone knew the secret of her birth but herself. When she'd confronted her parents she'd lashed out at them, too hurt to listen when they'd said they'd intended to tell her but had never found the right time. She'd screamed at them that she could never trust anyone again if she couldn't trust them. Only their obvious devastation at her words had tempered her anger.

Her parents had worked hard to win her trust back, to seek forgiveness, to assure her everything they'd done had been out of love for her. Eventually they had won her around. She was so glad she'd forgiven them, as her beloved father had died two years later of an unexpected heart attack. But she sometimes felt she was like a cracked vase that had been repaired but was never quite the same. There was a weaker seam running along that crack that had left her with a nagging distrust because the people closest to her had lied to her—and conspired to make sure she was oblivious to it.

When their waiter asked if they wanted another coffee, Eloise looked to Josh. He nodded. 'And another puppuccino for Daisy?' he asked.

'But of course,' she said, smiling. She was glad she'd have some more time with this thoughtful man. 'What line of business are you in?' she asked, to change the subject from the personal.

'Tech entrepreneur just about covers it. As

a teenager I started developing apps and trading gaming codes and went from there.'

'Clever you,' she said.

So he was smart as well as handsome. He wore a very expensive watch and his jacket and trousers were tailor-made from Italian fabrics. She figured he was about her age, so she could add *successful* to the list of his attributes.

'What about you?' he said.

'I'm a dress designer. Bridal wear mostly.'

'Always a market for that, I guess,' he said.

'Indeed,' she said.

But not for her. She made her living ensuring her clients' dreams of fairy-tale weddings came true. However, she had no intention of walking up the aisle herself any time soon.

Once, she'd been idealistic about the concept of romance, of falling in love at first sight the way her parents had—the story of their meeting at summer school had become family mythology—but those illusions had long been shattered. Perhaps because she had gone into her early relationships too ready to fall in love, and got too easily hurt and disillusioned as a result. These days she seemed to attract controlling men who hid behind superficial charm. Just because her business was 'girly'—their word—and she liked dressing in a feminine, vintage-inspired style didn't mean she wanted to be submissive. She'd escaped a difficult relationship a year ago and wasn't looking for another one.

'My gowns are exclusive and unique. I say without boasting that I have a long waiting list. Women in the know put their names down as soon as they think there's a chance of their guy proposing. Or their girl in the case of a same-sex couple.'

'It sounds a romantic way to make a living.'

She laughed. 'People often say that. Most of the time it is romantic and beautiful. To create an exquisite gown for a bride is a truly joyous thing. But have you heard the term Bridezilla?'

'Yes,' he said quickly. Too quickly. 'I… uh…have a friend who works in catering in Boston. She knows all about demanding Bridezillas.'

Eloise wondered how serious the 'friend' was and noted that he didn't wear a wedding band. It was just coffee, she reminded herself.

'The stress of organising a wedding can bring out the worst in people. Dream weddings can turn into nightmares.' She stopped herself. Okay, so she could get a touch cynical about happy-ever-afters that went wrong. But she would be wise to keep that level of detail to herself when she was chatting to a stranger.

Since she'd gone to Los Angeles and dressed the bride and eight attendants for the extravagant wedding of mega American pop star Roxee—the diva used only the one name—Eloise had been pestered for interviews. And learned how easy it was to be misquoted. She was very careful what she said now and never revealed anything confidential about a client.

'Thankfully Bridezillas are the exception,' she continued. 'Most brides are awesome and it's lovely to work with people at such a happy time of their lives. There's nothing I love more than being invited to their weddings. I go to mush and cry my eyes out every time.'

'Do you have a retail outlet? A factory?' She noticed he kept the conversation business-focused, which she liked. No disparaging 'girly' comments here, which she appreciated.

'Yes, to the store—no, to the factory. I have a storefront. In the window I display just one perfect dress that changes weekly. There are fitting rooms at that level. Upstairs is my atelier, which is a fancy name for a designer's workroom. But the French sounds classier, doesn't it?' She'd learned the term during her internship at a Paris couture bridal house.

'Branding is everything,' he said seriously.

'Eloise Evans Atelier works for me,' she said lightly. Her last boyfriend had been pushing her towards marriage. And expected that she would change her surname to his and her business name to reflect the change. *As if!*

She had worked too hard to build up her business, to make sure it was hers and hers alone, and no one would be allowed to take it from her.

'How long are you in Sydney?' she asked.

'Until tomorrow, then I fly to Melbourne,' he said. 'My time in Australia depends on how negotiations go with a start-up I want to buy.' She understood he would be tight-lipped about the details of his business. It must be highly competitive.

'I hope this lovely weather holds for the rest of your stay.'

The waiter came with their bill. In spite of the agreement that she would pay for the coffee, as he wouldn't let her pay for his dry cleaning, Josh went to pay for it. Eloise insisted she should pay. 'I invited you,' she said. 'Please.'

She didn't like it when men high-handedly insisted on paying, as it too often became a 'now you owe me' situation. Another way of them trying to assert control over her independence that she fiercely resisted. Not that she thought that would be the case with Josh. She suspected it was purely good manners on his part. Thankfully, he graciously conceded.

The waiter took their empty coffee cups away and an awkward silence fell between them that Eloise struggled to break. The sounds of the park—the clatter of cutlery in the café, Daisy's breathing—became something intrusive.

They spoke at the same time.

'I have to go—' she said.

'Would it be out of order to—?'

'To what?' She held her breath for his answer.

'Ask if you're free for dinner tonight?'

She didn't know who was more surprised, Josh or her at her rapid reply. 'Yes,' she said. 'I mean no, it wouldn't be at all out of order.'

CHAPTER THREE

JOSH COULDN'T BLAME the dog, or Eloise, or anyone else but himself for his spontaneous dinner invitation. At that moment, the need to see Eloise again while he was in town had overwhelmed good sense.

It had nothing to do with Tori or his self-appointed role of investigator. Fact was, he had enjoyed every second in Eloise's company and didn't want to say goodbye. There was something about her that fascinated him—and it wasn't just the resemblance to his friend. It had been a long time since he'd anticipated a date with such enthusiasm. And because he was a visitor in town only briefly, the encounter could be contained to just the one evening without there being any expectations of further dates. It could be awkward explaining to women that he didn't want the complication of commitment at this stage of his life.

But his obligation to Tori *was* a complication. Back in his hotel in Double Bay, not far from Eloise's atelier, he paced the room as he thought about what he would say to Tori. The time distance between Sydney and Boston meant late morning in Sydney was late evening back home. She would be anxiously waiting for his report on his sighting of her Australian lookalike, but he was curiously reluctant to speak to his friend. His reactions to the woman who must surely be Tori's long-lost twin were too new, too unexpected, too *private* for him to be interrogated or teased in best female friend style.

Josh wasn't a man to draw out decisions. He'd got where he was by being decisive, and acting swiftly on a mix of intuition and canny market knowledge. Yet he here was being indecisive as hell. Over a woman.

He knew that he could not lie to his friend about actually engaging with Eloise, sharing a coffee with her, arranging to see her again. Loyalty was important to him. In a world when even his own mother had ultimately proved disloyal, Tori and her family had been unfailingly loyal to him.

He picked up the phone. Tori reacted to his news with predictable excitement, demanding to know every detail twice over. The possible finding of a long-lost sister was a big deal and he knew it. He had lost a sibling, through unmitigated selfishness and greed on his brother's part, but it was a loss all the same and had left a brother-sized gap in his life. If Tori chose to make contact with Eloise she would find a kind person as besotted with dogs as she was. That could only be a blessing.

He recounted the incident with the dog and her ball and how it had brought him into accidental contact with Eloise. He told her they'd had coffee, how he was convinced the two women must be twins. And that even though they'd grown up separated from the age of two they had a lot in common and he was convinced Tori would like Eloise a lot. Fortunately, she didn't seem to pick up anything from his tone that revealed his unexpected and overwhelming attraction to Eloise.

Tori sniffed back tears. She thanked him effusively for tracking Eloise down for her. He told her he was seeing Eloise for dinner and she didn't object. Not that her objection would have stopped him. But he agreed again not to tell Eloise about Tori just yet.

As soon as he put down the phone he realised how difficult he had made things for himself. If at some stage the twins met each other, he would be the bad guy for not having told Eloise the truth straight away. Immediately he dismissed the thought. Surely Eloise would see he had done the right thing by staying silent about his real purpose for being in the park this morning. It was Tori's story to reveal, not his. He hoped she'd take action on it sooner rather than later.

He turned his mind to his work. From when he'd first started in his line of business he'd had dealings with people from all around the world and, while much of his business was conducted online, he liked to meet people face to face. His personal touch had won him business others had missed out on. He was tough in negotiations, but always fair. The ideal was that all parties to the transaction walked away from the negotiating table believing they'd got a good deal. That way led to ongoing, profitable business relationships. The end game was, after all, profit. Every new million he made was a kick in the teeth for the father and brother who had written him off as unworthy.

With recent world events, however, flights to Australia had been disrupted, so the point of this trip was to touch base with people he hadn't seen for far too long. But when an important client of his digital app marketplace called with a suggestion to meet for dinner that night he straight away declined the invitation. Then took a pause when he realised it was the first time he'd put a date with a woman ahead of a business deal.

Eloise had arranged for Josh Taylor to meet her at a favourite restaurant in nearby Potts Point. As her mother might say, it was wise to stay cautious about a man she had picked up in the park. No matter how genuine he seemed or how attractive she found him.

She'd quickly searched him online, of course—just enough to check if he was who he'd said he was—only to find he'd been remarkably self-effacing about his achievements. At twenty-nine, he was considered to be one of the world's leading tech moguls. He also appeared in several lists of 'most eligible bachelors' in the United States. Who knew? And she'd thought him just a friendly fellow dog lover. She could have read up on him all day but she'd had to rush into work.

But she made sure she and Daisy got back to her apartment in time for her to dress carefully for her date with Josh. Could she call it an actual date? He'd probably only suggested dinner because otherwise he'd be facing an evening alone in his hotel room and she was a friendly face. And that was okay because otherwise she would be curled up on the sofa, with Daisy at her feet, binge-watching TV.

But it didn't hurt to look her best. Despite its population of more than five million, Sydney was a small town—the eastern suburbs especially—and she never knew who she might see when she was out. Reputation was vital in her business and she couldn't be seen to be dressed anything less than stylishly. Not that it was a hardship. She adored dressing up and wearing make-up.

Tonight she was trialling one of her own designs, a heavy silk, full-skirted, calf-length nineteen-fifties-style dress in a flattering deep rose that she thought would be a hit for bridesmaids at a day-time wedding. She had a particular Bridezilla in mind, one who had told her she had directed her bridesmaids to lose weight so they'd all fit into the same size dresses.

This dress required a trim waist, so might work for those particular attendants. She'd had to use all her diplomatic skills not to retort that if she were a bridesmaid, she would immediately resign from bridesmaid's duties if any bride ever ordered her to lose weight, get a boob job, dye her hair to the wedding approved colour, or sign an agreement not to get pregnant before the bride's big day.

Eloise had heard them all. And every time was surprised at the women who went along with the crazy directives. Yet the perfect dress for the bride and for her attendants was a pivotal part of any wedding. It was her role to help every bride achieve her dream—the ideal gown for her fairy-tale wedding. What the bride and the bridesmaids did themselves wasn't Eloise's concern.

That wasn't a conversation she'd have with Josh over dinner though. Part of her success came from the fact that she always maintained strict confidentiality about her clients. Despite her design credentials, she would never have got the Roxee gig without her reputation for being scrupulous about her clients' privacy. She'd had no qualms about signing the strict non-disclosure agreements, and both before and after Roxee's wedding she had refused substantial sums to dish the dirt on what happened behind the scenes at celebrity weddings. In interviews she spoke about the thrill of working for the stars, snippets about her design process, but nothing that hadn't been cleared by her clients. Her business would soon dry up if she was indiscreet. And she fiercely protected her business. It was something that was all her own and that gave her a certain sense of security in a world that had been turned upside down when she was thirteen and had never quite spun on the same axis again.

Eloise was proud of what she had achieved. From making gorgeous original prom dresses for her friends at high school, to creating exclusive wedding dresses for clients including international superstars, her business brought her independence and fulfilment and she loved it.

The early days of her career, working in established fashion houses, had made her all the more determined to strike out with her own business, where she wouldn't be answerable to anyone. One well-known name had taken credit for her designs and then fired her when she'd asked for some acknowledgement—apparently all her work was his intellectual property and it said so in the contract she hadn't properly read. She'd resigned from another who used cheap materials but charged huge prices to the bride. With her own busi-

ness she could work the way she wanted—
and if it failed she could only blame herself.
She'd worked hard to make Eloise Evans Atelier the success it was. She would do anything
to protect it. How a man could expect her to
give it up or let him take a hand in its man-
agement was beyond her. And that was what
the most recent man in her life had expected
her to do if she'd married him.

She should have seen the warning signs
flashing around Craig sooner than she had.
He'd been very good-looking and she'd fallen
right back into that instant attraction trap.
She'd been infatuated with him in the beginning and stupidly blinded to the reality of the
man until finally her self-preservation mech-
anisms had kicked in. But not before he had
inflicted serious damage to her self-esteem.

Craig had drip-fed criticisms of her—
sometimes in the guise of barbed compli-
ments or 'helpful' advice—until she had
started doubting herself, censoring her answers to him so they wouldn't annoy him.
He had pressed for an engagement but some
deep instinct held her back. One day he had
gone to kiss her and she hadn't wanted to kiss
him back. Not then. Not ever. When she'd finally broken up with him, he had shown his

true colours in a stream of invective that had shattered her. Then she found out he'd been cheating on her. No wonder she had soured on the idea of marriage. No wonder those old feelings of not being able to trust anyone close to her had resurfaced.

Fortunately, she'd then been plunged into the distracting workload of Roxee's wedding, which had involved several trips to LA, and there'd been no time for her to date.

Josh had arrived at the restaurant before Eloise. As she came in she saw him sitting at the table he'd booked, head down as he scrolled through his phone. She took the opportunity to admire him. The man was every bit as hot as she remembered. And as well dressed. Sophisticated in a lightweight charcoal sweater—cashmere, she was sure—with the sleeves pushed up to reveal that bank-balance-defying watch, and black linen trousers.

After the Craig fiasco more than a year ago, she hadn't dated at all. Casual dinners with trusted male friends only. She was surprised at how content she was being single. It meant she could live her life on her terms, could work all hours without being accused of not giving her man enough attention. Or having to worry what he might be up to while she had to work—a particular kind of worry she could well do without.

Of course, sometimes she got lonely for a man's company, a man's arms around her. Just that morning when she'd set off for her walk with Daisy she'd realised with a pang just how many couples there were in the park, from teenagers entwined around each other to silver-haired seniors holding hands. For a moment she'd felt suddenly alone in a world of couples. Until Daisy had sniffed out another single, quite probably the most attractive man in the park. And here he was now, waiting for her in her favourite restaurant. A casual, no-strings date with a handsome man might be just the lift her spirits needed.

He looked up, saw her, and smiled. Her eyes connected with his and for a long moment the noises surrounding them—the clatter of cutlery, the murmur of conversation—faded away. The shimmering thread of awareness drawing her to him seemed almost tangible until, flustered, she gave a shaky smile back and headed to the table. *What was happening here?*

The admiration in his eyes as he rose to greet her assured her that the pink dress had been a good choice. She'd teamed it with a lacy knit vintage cardigan in a paler shade of pink embellished with silver beading and wore her favourite silver stilettos.

'You look lovely,' he said. 'One of your own creations?'

'But of course,' she said, preening just a little.

She took her seat opposite him, settling her full skirts around her. They ordered first drinks and then their meals. There wasn't any of the awkwardness of a first date. She marvelled at how she slipped into conversation with him as easily as she had at the park.

'Where's Daisy?' he asked, pretending to look around for a dog.

'Did you expect me to bring her?'

'It would have been nice to see her again,' he said with an obvious sincerity that pleased her. Craig had pretended to like dogs until he'd felt more certain of her. Then he'd let slip that he would never allow her to have a dog after they were married. *Allow* her! That might have been the moment her feelings for him had started to turn.

'She's safely asleep at my apartment, all tired out from her run in the park and then a visit to my workroom, where the staff all make a fuss of her.'

'You take your dog to work with you?'

'The advantage of being the boss. Of course, we have to keep her away from the expensive fabrics and laces we have in the workroom. Other foster dogs I've had haven't been as easy as this little one. She's happy to be crated if need be.'

'Do you usually work weekends?'

She leaned across the table towards him. 'I work any day I need to. Weekends suit some clients better. I like to do the final fitting for a bride whenever I can rather than leave it to one of my staff.'

'So I'm having drinks with a perfectionist?'

'Some say workaholic.' She laughed. 'I don't mind which label you use. There's a lot of hope and dreams invested in a wedding dress and I want that dress to look as perfect as it possibly can on my bride so she feels confident and comfortable.'

'There are a lot of dollars invested in your gowns too.'

'We use only the finest fabrics and trims; they don't come cheap.' She paused. 'How do you know how much my gowns cost?' She put up her hand in a halt sign. 'Wait. I get it. You looked me up online.'

'Of course.' He paused for a beat. 'Didn't you do a search on me?'

'Er…yes. Seems you own half the digital world. You were remarkably modest about your achievements.' She wouldn't say anything about the eligible bachelor lists that seemed to haunt his internet presence.

'So were you. *Bridal wear designer to the stars.* You don't get more famous than Roxee.'

'I know.' She grinned. 'I was positively star-struck when she got in touch. But she's a lovely, warm person and was wonderful to deal with. Her fabulous wedding and her commendations of my label have been brilliant for me. Business went ballistic. I've had to take on more staff and be prepared to fly more often to the US for personal fittings for her celebrity friends.'

Eloise waited for him to ask for inside gossip on the mega star—as so many people had since the wedding—and was relieved when he didn't. She would have thought less of him.

'It seems the designer became famous too.'

'Not really. It's second-hand fame, isn't it? I don't like being in the spotlight. I'm a backroom girl. I find interviews excruciating.'

'I don't care for the spotlight either, except when it serves my purposes,' he said shortly. 'My personal life is my own business.' She was glad she hadn't mentioned the eligible bachelor thing.

The waiter came with their starters—organic Sydney rock oysters for him and a salad of seared, cured trout for her.

'How did you get to be a wedding dress designer to the stars?' he asked when she had finished her salad.

'I'll ignore that label, if you don't mind,' she said, with a smile. 'I'm just as happy working with a girl from the suburbs who's saved up for one of my dresses, and gets to be a star for a day at her wedding.'

'Seriously,' he said, putting down his tiny oyster fork. 'When you were a little girl, did you say "I'm going to grow up and design wedding gowns for international superstars"?'

'Actually, I said I was going to grow up to be a mermaid.'

He laughed. 'Cute.'

'I don't know why, as I'm not a particularly keen swimmer. I think it was the idea of having a glorious tail, glistening with multicoloured scales. Which, when you think of it, is not so different from a bride's glorious long train trailing after her as she glides her way up the aisle, picking up the light from the beautiful beading and crystals stitched onto it.'

'You're obviously highly creative,' he said, a smile twitching around the corner of his mouth. 'And imaginative.'

'Even as a little girl I loved colour and texture and fabrics. Most of all I loved clothes. My grandmother—my Australian grandmother, that is—was no fashionista but she taught me basic sewing and I stitched garments for my dolls as soon as I could use scissors and needles and thread. The same grandmother gave me a sewing machine for my eleventh birthday and I started making my own clothes. I was a puzzle to my mother. She's a scientist with, as she herself says, no real interest in fashion. She lets me choose her clothes for her now, which is fun.'

His eyes narrowed. 'So you don't take after your parents.'

She shrugged. 'I don't, and maybe I do. I'm the creative one in a family of intellectuals and scientists. But I'm adopted, so that's no great surprise.'

Every time she told people she was adopted she forced her voice to sound calm and even, as if it were no big deal. And maybe it wouldn't seem a big deal if she'd been told she was adopted from the get-go. But she would never forget the shock of discovering the hidden truth of her birth. The justification of that nagging feeling that she somehow didn't fit, the creative in the family of pragmatic academics. She had the same colouring as her father, so no one had ever doubted she was their birth child. But that shock, that feeling of betrayal and mistrust, was burned deep into her psyche.

'I don't know anything about my birth family except my birth mother worked in a department store, so maybe she was into fashion too,' she said.

Both she and her adoptive parents had tried to find out more, but with no luck. After a while, she'd asked them to stop the search. It seemed painful and pointless, especially when she had decided to forgive her parents for their deception and embrace the family who had chosen her rather than abandoned her.

Sometimes, when she sent one of her foster dogs off to their new home with a sense of satisfaction he or she would now get the good life they deserved, she wondered about the social worker who had placed her with the Evans family. Was that how it had felt for them, for the adoption agency, to place an unwanted little girl with a loving family who would care for her as if she were their own?

Always, she forced those thoughts to the back of her mind. To know she'd been unwanted was too hurtful. No one on either side of her birth parents' families had claimed her after her birth mother's death. Sometimes she rationalised that her adoptive maternal grandmother had made up for all those others who hadn't wanted her, but their rejection still stung deep down. No matter how exceptionally fortunate she had been with her adoptive parents.

'What about your birth father?'

'Father unknown,' she said making light of it by forming quote marks with her fingers. She wasn't telling him anything that she hadn't spoken about in interviews in the past.

'I'm sorry,' he said.

'Don't be. I couldn't imagine a better father than my real—that is, my adoptive—father was to me. Or my amazing mother, who did her very best to nurture and encourage the cuckoo she had brought into her nest.' Not that her mother had ever called her a cuckoo—that was Eloise's own term, devised to explain her role in the Evans family. 'She tells me it was an adventure to see how I would turn out. According to her, it was like seeing a flower bud unfurl, blossoming into possibilities that my pragmatic parents had never imagined.'

That was the truth. Except some of that had been recognised in retrospect. After she'd come to terms with the truth of her adoption, after she had struggled with her identity. After she had vowed to be the best daughter she could be to the people who had rescued her.

Josh raised his eyebrows. 'And you don't think your mother is creative? That's quite an analogy.'

'She's rather proud of her story, I think. But I never tire of hearing it. It's only as an adult that I truly appreciated how generous she was. She says I must have got my creativity from my first mother, the woman to whom she was so grateful. She couldn't have children of her own.'

One of the worst times in the six months of rebellion and trauma that had followed the discovery of the adoption document, had been when her mother had cried as she'd explained how much she loved her, what a gift she'd been to a mother who could not conceive a child of her own.

'Your parents sound great.' There was an edge to Josh's voice Eloise couldn't place.

She nodded. 'I was fortunate. I was cherished and loved and encouraged to follow my own interests in art and design. I won a dress-designing competition in a teen magazine when my dad was still alive. He said he couldn't have been more proud of me than if I'd been awarded a doctorate.'

'Sounds like the perfect childhood,' he said. 'If such a thing exists.'

She toyed with her linen napkin. 'Do I sound ungrateful if I say it was *nearly* perfect? There was always something missing.' She acknowledged her adoption to wonderful parents, but this was something she didn't often talk about. It had nothing to do with her adoption, and everything to do with her personal wishes. But there was no harm in it. His calm, accepting manner made it easy to open up.

'What was that?' he said.

'A sister. I longed for a sister. Not a brother, although I liked boys. I used to beg my mother to give me a sister. I was so sure of the sister I wanted, I drew a picture of her when I was about seven. My mother laughed when I handed her my sketch; she said I'd drawn an image of myself. She's still got it.'

Josh made a strangled sound that might have been a cough, suppressed laughter, or some kind of choking attack. Silently, she passed his water glass towards him. 'That's amusing,' he said finally, after he'd drunk some water. 'That you'd drawn a self-portrait, I mean.' She got the feeling he didn't find it amusing at all, but she couldn't imagine why.

The waiter brought their main courses. Eloise welcomed the interruption. She felt she'd talked far too much about herself without finding out anything much about him. He was dangerously easy to confide in.

Once she had tasted her favourite dish at the restaurant, a pan-fried chicken breast finished with truffle oil, and asked Josh how his steak was, she put down her knife and fork. Time to redress the balance.

'Do you have a sister or brother?' she asked. 'Or both?'

He paused for a beat too long before he spoke. 'How deeply did you burrow into the search engine when you looked me up?'

'I only had a quick look because I had to get to work. I figured if you really were a tech entrepreneur as you said, there would be something there on you beyond the usual social media. I didn't expect to find thousands of pages.'

'Did you read about the so-called scandal?'

'Not that I recall.'

She would certainly have remembered something *scandalous*. She shifted in her seat. Was Josh what he appeared to be? Her instincts were finely honed when it came to her business. Not so reliable when it came to men. Somehow she wanted to believe the best of Josh, but was that just because she found him so attractive? No, Daisy had trusted him too. Another day a good-looking man had come close to them in the park and Daisy had whimpered her fear then flattened her ears and bared her teeth at him. Eloise had walked briskly away—the complete opposite of what had happened with Josh.

'If I don't tell you you'll look it up as soon as you get home, won't you?' he said wryly.

'I might do just that,' she said lightly. 'You can't throw out the word *scandal* and not expect people to bite.'

'Fair enough,' he said. 'I guess I'll have to follow through.'

She groaned. 'Please stop dangling the bait. You've really got me intrigued now.'

Josh took a sip of his wine and settled back into his chair. His tension betrayed itself by his tight grip on the glass. What was the scandal he was about to reveal? Would it send her running from the restaurant?

'Like you, I had what might seem to be an idyllic childhood. I was born into one of the best families in Boston. A mansion on Beacon Hill. An illustrious heritage stretching back generations. A predetermined place in society. A big brother six years older than me who I looked up to. A father, distant but caring in his own way in that I lacked for nothing. A loving mother. However, also like you, I sometimes felt like the cuckoo in the nest. My brother seemed to excel in everything expected of him to take the path into the family's long-established legal firm. But I was a constant disappointment to my father. I'd rather have been on the sports field than in the library, although maths and computing came easily. I questioned rather than accepted the way things "had always been done".'

'Surely there's room for a rebel in every family?'

Again that wry smile. 'Rebel, perhaps. Interloper, definitely not.'

She frowned. 'What do you mean by interloper?'

'At the age of sixteen, a routine blood test proved I could not be my father's son.' Eloise gasped. 'All hell exploded at home. My mother confessed to an affair. Both she and I were expelled from the family.'

Eloise stared at him. 'I… I don't know what to say. Except that it sounds more a tragedy than a scandal.'

'You and I might say that; others didn't, I can assure you.'

Aching with sympathy, she leaned closer over the table. She longed to put her hand over his but didn't think it would be appropriate or welcome. 'It must have been terrible for you.' Just as traumatic as finding out she'd been adopted.

'You could say that,' he said with the understatement she was beginning to realise was part of him. 'My father—the only father I had ever known and who I loved—wanted nothing to do with me. I was forbidden to use the family name, banned from the family home and disinherited. He never paid another cent of support.' His words were underscored with bitterness.

Eloise's meal sat abandoned. She could only concentrate on the man sitting opposite her. The downward pull of his mouth, his set jaw, betrayed he was still struggling to come to terms with an old hurt. 'That seems unbelievably cruel.'

'I'd always known he was a hard man. But not that hard. He was furious he'd been fooled into bringing up another man's son. It appeared his relationship with me was collateral damage.'

'I can see he would have been angry. After all, his wife had lied to him in a major way. But to take it out on an innocent kid seems appalling. Who was your biological father?'

Since she'd discovered she was adopted, this kind of terminology came easily to her.

'My mother's tennis coach. She says she was in love, but that it was just a fling to him. He moved on. She wasn't sure I was his until after I was born. Luckily for my mother, I looked like her and no one questioned my legitimacy. But she could see her lover in me. When she tried to contact him, it was to find he'd died in a mountaineering accident. His family never knew about me.

My mother never revealed my birth father's name—it was scandal enough that my father had disowned me. Even though she wasn't happy with my father, she stayed.'

'For your sake?'

'And for my brother's, she says. But she also liked the good life my father provided. She didn't come from a wealthy family.'

Eloise frowned. 'That sounds harsh.'

'Even she admits it was true. Although she told me she felt so guilty about deceiving him, she strove to be the perfect wife to a difficult man she didn't love to make up for her deception.'

'No one else knew the facts of your birth?'

'She hugged her secret to herself for sixteen years.'

'Your mother must have been on tenterhooks the entire time that she'd be caught out.' Had her parents even considered the possibility she would find out the truth about her adoption before they chose to tell her?

'With good cause. Her husband's reaction was swift and brutal. He's had no further contact with me since the day he booted me out.'

She noticed she didn't call his mother's husband his father. The hurt must run deep and bitter. He wouldn't trust easily either. 'What about your brother? Surely he stood up for you? Not that you'd done anything wrong.'

Josh pulled down his mouth in a grimace. 'He sided with my father. Why not when one day he'll get the entirety rather than half of a massive inheritance? He had a personal grudge too. When the scandal erupted he reckoned it ruined his chances of going into politics.'

'He blamed you? A teenager?'

'I was an easy target.'

'It all sounds terribly unfair.'

'I got through it all right,' he said, tight-lipped.

'You certainly have,' she said.

In terms of wealth and success anyway. In terms of personal damage, who knew how it had affected him? She remembered how vulnerable she had been at sixteen, determined to be an adult, to take risks, but buoyed by the security and guidance of her mother there for her. And, before he died, her father's loving support. 'Thank you for sharing that with me.'

He shrugged. 'I haven't told you anything that's not public knowledge—it's still often brought up in stories about my success. I thought I should clear the air in case you'd read about it.'

But she knew there must be so much more to it. 'I can understand, in a way, how you felt when you discovered the truth.'

'Really?' She could tell by the narrowing of his eyes he didn't believe anyone could ever understand what he'd been through.

'I didn't discover I was adopted until I was thirteen. And then it was only by accident.'

He frowned. 'Your parents hadn't told you?'

She shook her head. 'They said they nearly did on so many occasions but didn't know how to. They're highly intelligent people, so I don't quite get that, but there it is. I imagine you might have gone through some of the same struggles with identity as I did.' Only she had had parents who genuinely loved her to help her through it.

'You could say that, yes,' he said. 'I was sixteen, a kid, but savvy enough to realise what had happened. Why I hadn't fitted the family mould suddenly became clear.'

'For me too. Although I was lucky and my family embraced my differences.'

'Two different situations. Your parents

chose you. My father felt I was foisted on him. He hated me for it.'

'Hate. That's a harsh word.'

'I was a kid of sixteen. A boy that age shouldn't have to learn to hate back. But I did.' His face was set in grim lines but she could see traces of the bewilderment he must have felt as a teenager.

'I'm sorry,' she said.

He shrugged again. 'In one way it was the making of me. I forged a new life in a different part of town, where no one cared where I'd fallen from. Forced into earning my own living to help my mother, I grew up quickly. Almost immediately I started refurbishing unwanted mobile phones and selling them on at a profit, all while I was still in high school.'

'You had to prove him wrong about you,' she said softly, gaining a glimmering of understanding of what it had been like for him.

'Correct,' he said.

She wondered why they were talking in such depth like this, as if it was a first date and there would be others. That wasn't going to happen.

He'd mentioned earlier that he would be flying down to Melbourne the next day, then flying back to Boston from there. There was an undeniable attraction between them—she could almost see the sparks. But it could go nowhere. She felt sad about that; it wasn't often she felt as comfortable with a man.

But she lived in Sydney and he in Boston. When she was nineteen, she'd snagged an internship in Paris working with a couture bridal house. She'd fallen crazily in love with a French guy and he with her. It had been real, not just a fling. After she'd gone back to Sydney, they'd tried to keep up the relationship long distance, but it had proved too difficult. It would be too difficult now. She reined in her thoughts. This was just one date. No one was considering romance, let alone a long-distance relationship.

'I'm glad I heard about the scandal from you rather than through an internet search,' she said. 'But I still say it's a tragedy.'

The waiter appeared at the table to ask if she and Josh had finished their meals. They looked at each other and laughed. 'We've been talking too much.'

'And I've enjoyed every minute of it,' Josh said, his voice deep and husky.

So had she. She didn't want the evening to end. And she hadn't felt like that for a long, long time.

* * *

Josh walked Eloise to her car. Purposely he took slow steps to extend his time with her for as long as possible. He didn't hold her hand, put his arm around her, or brush his shoulder against hers, although he wanted to. He gritted his teeth against the urge to pull her into his arms. She was gloriously sexy in that glamorous dress, although this rush of attraction was about so much more than that.

The way she tilted her head at a slight angle as she listened to him—really listened to him—and understood. Her wholehearted laugh. How that laughter reflected in those remarkable eyes, cornflower-blue fringed with thick black lashes that must be fake or enhanced with make-up, because he hadn't noticed them in the park. The lushness of her mouth slicked with deep red lipstick with a boldness that was almost theatrical. The sparkle of her creativity—she'd had him halfway to wishing he had a merman's tail. *Him*. Josh Taylor, who had no time for fanciful flights of imagination unless it led to something marketable and profitable. And yet the professionalism in the way she spoke about the business she was so passionate about had also struck a chord. In that drive to succeed, they were like-minded.

She and Tori might look alike but Eloise was entirely her own person. The whole evening he hadn't given Tori a thought. Except when Eloise had mentioned the way she'd sketched herself as an indication of her ideal sister and he'd nearly choked on his surprise. Apart from that, he hadn't remarked to himself on their similarities or their differences. Because Eloise was Eloise.

And he liked her, really liked her. But he had made a promise to Tori not to tell Eloise about their connection. If he took his interest in Eloise any further he would find himself tangled in a net of deception. That was not something he felt comfortable with. Not something Eloise would appreciate either, he was sure, even with his limited knowledge of her.

If he was wise, he would forget any further contact with Eloise until the day Tori could explain how he had acted as an advance scout in her search for her twin—and, short of DNA testing, he was convinced they *were* twins— and they could have a good laugh about the way Daisy had engineered their meeting.

Apart from that, he wasn't in the market

for a serious relationship. Not now. Maybe not ever. And Eloise had commitment and permanence written all over her beautiful self. How could he possibly fool around with Tori's sister? Tori might have been adopted into an Italian family but those Italian expectations of family loyalty she held were real and ran very deep in her. If he dated her sister, she would expect nothing short of a proposal. No. He would be wise to keep a very, very wide berth from this gorgeous woman.

They reached Eloise's car, a vintage Scandinavian sports car circa 1962, a collector's item in immaculate condition. A woman with a cool car. His admiration for her rocketed even higher. Eloise turned to face him, car keys dangling from her hand.

'Thank you. Dinner was an unexpected surprise and I enjoyed it very much.'

'I hope we can keep in touch,' he said. They had swapped numbers that morning in the park.

'I'd like that,' she said. Her voice was cool and contained and gave him no hint as to whether she really wanted to see him again or was being polite. It was just one date and they both knew it.

He would urge Tori to get in touch with

Eloise soon, and give her the sister she'd sketched all those years ago. And let Eloise give Tori her imaginary friend for real.

'Next time you come to the States for one of your celebrity clients, perhaps you can swing by Boston,' he said.

'It's a thought,' she said, again polite and non-committal.

She stood half in shadow but as she looked up at him the movement took her into the warm glow of a street light. Her eyes shone incredibly blue and the rich red lipstick gleamed on her luscious mouth. 'Goodbye, then,' she said.

'Goodbye,' he echoed.

But he couldn't break the irresistible pull of her gaze. He had felt it in the restaurant when he had first noticed she had arrived, an attraction so powerful it had transcended the space between them. Now she stood so close he was aware of her warmth, her tantalising scent. There were no further words to be said. The silence that hung between them could only be broken in one way.

He lowered his head to kiss her as she stepped closer to accept his kiss. He realised he had wanted this since the moment she'd laughed up at him in the park, had wanted to push his fingers through her thick hair. He did that now and she gave a little murmur of pleasure. Then he kissed her on her mouth. After an initial start of surprise, she kissed him back wholeheartedly. What started as a sweet and tender goodnight kiss flamed into something urgent and passionate that overtook him with its intensity. For minutes, or it could have been hours, all he was aware of was Eloise—her taste, her warmth, the excitement of having her in his arms.

But then, with a little sigh of regret, she broke away from the kiss, stepped back from him, her face flushed, her lips swollen, her hair in delicious disarray. 'That... that shouldn't have happened.' Her voice wasn't steady as she tried to control her erratic breathing.

His voice was hoarse. 'I'm glad it did.' He put his hand on her shoulder, suddenly unable to bear the loss of her touch.

She gave a shaky smile. 'I don't do one-night stands—'

'I didn't expect—'

She put a finger across his lips to silence him. 'We both know what we'll want if we keep on kissing like that. We both know what would happen if I invited you into my car and back to my flat.' She paused to drag in air, and her breasts rose in a way he found almost unbearably alluring. 'Not a good idea,' she said.

She was so beautiful.

'No,' he choked out, while his body screamed *yes.* She wriggled out of his reach. Reluctantly, he let her go.

'Thank you, Josh, for a wonderful evening— I enjoyed every minute.' She flashed him a mischievous smile. 'Especially the last few minutes.'

He laughed and any awkwardness evaporated. 'Goodbye, Eloise.'

She swung her long, shapely legs into her car. It suited her, its era, her style. With just one backward glance and a fleeting smile, she drove away with a throaty roar of the engine. He watched the sleek, small white car until it turned a corner, raising his hand in a final, farewell wave he knew she couldn't see.

CHAPTER FOUR

DESPITE HIS RESOLVE, Josh could not get Eloise out of his mind. When had he ever met a more enchanting woman? Her lovely face, her warm laugh, their sensational kiss all haunted his thoughts. Why did it have to be so damn complicated?

Boy meets girl. Girl is most likely boy's friend's long-lost twin, but boy is honour-bound not to reveal his connection. Girl lives on the other side of the world. Boy does not want to be distracted by girl while he still has goals he has to fulfil. But boy is distracted no matter how he tries not to think about girl.

Man, was he distracted.

Josh particularly found his thoughts turning to Eloise while at the most important of his Melbourne meetings—with Courtney and Shawn, the people behind the phenomenally successful digital graphic design platform he had invested heavily in as a start-up. It had been one of his best decisions, as it had also brought him two good friends.

They were a couple, deeply in love and planning their wedding. He recommended Eloise Evans Atelier, only to be told by the delighted bride that she was already on the waiting list and his wedding invitation was in the mail. 'Plus one, of course.'

'Just keep it at me,' he said. 'No plus-one.'

Despite her not so subtle questioning, Josh did not enlighten her to the state of his love life. Nor did he allow Courtney—or Tori for that matter—to set him up with any of her single friends. His love life—or lack of it— was his own business.

His ex-father—what else could he call him?—and his ex-brother—ditto—had written him off as a future asset to the family firm from an early age. He had not fitted the mould. All the men in the family went to Harvard and Josh had had no desire to be a lawyer. His interests had lain in the digital world and a degree in computing. Then the truth of his parentage had come out and suddenly there had been no college fund, no support. He had been so shocked when the issue of his birth identity had erupted. 'But Dad—' he'd protested.

His father hadn't let him finish. 'Don't ever call me that again. I'm not your *dad*. You are nothing to do with me. You're the result of a sordid liaison between a deadbeat and a woman of dubious morals. I wipe my hands of you completely.'

His mother had gasped at that. But she hadn't tried to defend herself. Or him.

Even his high school girlfriend had dumped him when he'd been booted from the big house on Beacon Hill to live with his mother in his widowed aunt's apartment in the North End. He'd thought she'd been as in love with him as he'd been in love with her. Seemed it was the wealth and lifestyle he'd lost that had been the attraction.

That was when he'd started to grow the cynical shield around his heart that had now hardened into a barrier he liked to consider impenetrable. And he'd found truth in that old saying, *He who travels fastest, travels alone.*

'Perhaps you just haven't met the right woman yet,' Tori had been known to say.

But it wasn't that. His energy had to be put into proving to his ex-father and half-brother that, in terms of the material success their world judged people by, he not just matched but also exceeded them. He didn't want long-term relationships—and the emotional fall-out that came with them—to get in the way.

Despite the cramped quarters at Aunt Lil's apartment, the enforced move had been a revelation. Boston's Little Italy neighbourhood, with its crowded old buildings dating back to the very early days of the city, was lively and convivial. He'd met Tori and her brothers, Ty and Tate, at his new high school and found both a warm welcome and income-producing gigs as a waiter at the Italian restaurant Tori's parents ran.

He still considered their trattoria to be a home from home. It had been a welcome escape from his mother's misery and depression. Looking back, he realised how much it must have hurt her to lose her home and contact with her older son. Back then, Josh had thought she'd blamed him—or the accident of his birth—for it all. He'd been at the trattoria more than he'd been at home.

Today, Tuesday lunchtime, he was eating with his Melbourne friends at a small, family-run Thai restaurant in one of Melbourne's famous laneways. It had the same kind of casual warmth and excellent food as the trattoria—as well as off-the-beaten-track privacy. As far as Josh was concerned, the good thing about being successful in the digital world, as opposed to something more 'glamorous', was that he tended to fly under the radar when it came to media attention.

Lately, however, his rocketing wealth and single status had been getting him unwanted attention—and he didn't like it. He'd complained to the publications about his inclusion in puerile 'eligible bachelor' lists—which had only excited them into asking for interviews. What did his relationship status—or lack of it—have to do with anything?

But here, he could enjoy his anonymity with his friends. While the food was good and the company excellent, he couldn't help but be aware of the conspicuously empty chair at the four-person table. How would it be if Eloise sat there next to him? He'd never before met a woman he'd want to introduce to his friends.

Four successful young entrepreneurs would have a lot to chat about. He could imagine the spirited conversation, the laughter, the strong opinions tossed back and forth. The thought conjured up an image of her sitting there, smiling at him, holding his hand under the table. It almost seemed real. But the empty chair glared back at him.

The long lunch over, he farewelled his friends with promises of seeing them again at their wedding. Then he headed back to his luxurious suite in one of Melbourne's most stylish Southbank hotels. For several hours, he attended to the necessary phone and video-call catch-ups that being in a different time zone entailed. He had no more appointments for the day after those were complete though and now he was on his own.

Usually he valued time to himself. But this afternoon he only felt restless. And, unusually for him, lonely. Perhaps seeing Courtney and Shawn so happy together was affecting him. Making him think thoughts he usually pushed far to the back of his mind, to keep company with other repressed thoughts of love and family and the security of shared lives. *Not for him,* he reminded himself. Not now. He was only twenty-nine. Perhaps later. Much later.

He found himself looking out of the floor-to-ceiling windows over the winding Yarra River and the staggered skyline of a city that wasn't home. He flew back to Boston tomorrow. But he would be flying back to loneliness too, packing it in his bag and trans-porting it with him to his empty apartment. Being alone was the price he had willingly paid for the freedom to build his staggering wealth that disproved, dollar by dollar, that he hadn't been worthy of the family he'd been born into.

Boy could not forget girl.

Eloise intrigued him. He wanted to see her face again, hear her magical laugh. Just a friendly meeting. Not a date. No physical contact like kissing, which only complicated things. It made sense, didn't it, to act on that impulse when he was in the same country as her rather than half a world away?

Thoughts of her flashed through his mind: her uninhibited joy in her scruffy little fos-ter dog; the sensual sway when she walked in high-heeled shoes; the understanding in her eyes when he'd told her some of his past.

He started to text:

I find I have to be back in Sydney on Thursday. Would lunch be out of the question? Josh T

He pressed *send* and stared at the screen. She'd be busy in her workshop. Perhaps fit-ting a client. Maybe even dreaming up a spectacular dress for Courtney. But within seconds, the phone pinged a reply.

Nice to hear from you. Thursday is a busy day for me, but I'd like to catch up. A quick lunch would be great. Suggest a café near my atelier.

She texted the address of the café and a suggested time, to which Josh agreed.

He put down the phone and realised, to his surprise, that his hand wasn't quite steady and his heart was thudding.

But he had no time to think about what that meant. He had to reroute his flight home via Sydney. If he had to, he would hire a private jet.

CHAPTER FIVE

ELOISE COULDN'T HELP checking her watch
every few minutes. Josh should be here very
soon. She'd got to the café early, a favourite
lunch spot for her just diagonally over the
road from work. Her usual waitress, a lovely
girl named Mara, had shown her to a table
outside under the shade of an umbrella—it
was another perfect, sunny autumn day.

She was excited at the prospect of seeing
Josh again, while also filled with a healthy
dose of trepidation. That unexpected kiss had
aroused long dormant appetites and emotions.
It was true what she'd told him—she wasn't
a one-night stand kind of girl. Yet once her
car had turned the corner and he'd fallen out
of sight, she'd had to fight the urge to turn it
around with a screech of tyres, speed back
and tell him to jump in the car. Her place

or his hotel—it wouldn't have mattered once they'd got hot and naked.

She had to fan her face with her hand at the very thought. Obviously she'd been too long without a man to be having fantasies like that about someone she hardly knew. Yet Josh had not been far from her thoughts since she'd driven away from him. She found him hotter than hot—especially after that kiss—but she had also really enjoyed his company.

There was a straightforwardness to him she found refreshing. And she'd liked his kindness to Daisy, which she was convinced was genuine. Dogs didn't lie and Daisy had approved of him. She had been surprised and pleased when he'd texted on Tuesday. But he still lived in a country that was, at best, a twenty-one-hour flight away. Hardly conducive to dating.

However, dating and all the drama that went with it wasn't at the front of her mind right now. Since she'd had that text from Josh her world had imploded.

She really should have cancelled the lunch and concentrated on trying to put the social media fires out. But she wanted to see him, and who knew when lunch with Josh would happen again, if ever? For that reason, she decided not to share the story of the disaster that had erupted yesterday. Rather she would push it down under a cheerful façade to be the trouble-free woman he had dined with just a few days ago. She was used to solving her own problems. Although this particular nightmare might not be easily solved—and the impact on her business could be considerable.

She looked up, saw him striding towards her table and caught her breath. Josh in a dark charcoal, perfectly tailored business suit rocketed his degree of hotness to blow the top off the thermometer. She used to think tech people, no matter how wealthy, hung out in hoodies and sneakers. Josh was the sartorially splendid exception. She couldn't remember when she'd last found a man so attractive.

He got to the table and she rose to greet him on legs that felt suddenly shaky. She looked up at him, his lean, strikingly good-looking face seeming already familiar. His nose, slightly crooked, saved him from being pretty-boy handsome, and his dark brown hair cut short seemed to resent being tamed, going off in rebellious spikes. And his mouth, his sensual mouth, his top lip slightly narrower than the bottom… A shiver of desire ran through her at the remembered pleasure of his kiss.

But she didn't trust that kind of instant attraction. Handsome Craig had hidden so well what kind of man he really was. She'd been like an insect, lured by the sweetness of honey, only to find herself sinking in a heavy, suffocating mass. Thank heaven she'd found the strength to struggle to the top and then fly away. When she next got into a relationship it would only be after a long getting-to-know-him process. She needed to embrace her feelings of mistrust towards men, not fight them. Only time could build trust.

But that kiss had happened and it seemed to make a handshake in greeting redundant. She looked up at Josh for a long moment, not sure what to do. He had no such hesitation. He claimed her mouth for a quick, warm kiss of greeting. 'Glad you were free for lunch,' he said.

She had to fight the temptation to raise her fingers to her lips, tingling with the pleasure of his touch. Even a simple kiss sent a shiver of awareness reverberating through her.

Then Mara the waitress was there again. She looked from Josh to Eloise and back again. 'Good to see you here again, sir,' she said to Josh with a big smile. 'So it was *her* you were waiting for.'

Eloise wasn't sure what Mara meant. Had Josh got here before her then gone again? It was possible.

Josh was quick to explain. 'I'm staying near by at the same hotel I stayed at last week. I came here for coffee then. When I got here, I was surprised to find it was the same café.'

'I see,' she said, not sure it was a full explanation but shrugging it off as nothing to worry about. She had enough real issues to worry about without angsting over imagined ones.

She sat down and he sat down opposite her. It was a table for two, so that wasn't far between them. She had to purposely angle her legs not to come into contact with his legs. When they accidentally brushed together, jolts of awareness reminded her of how she had felt when he had kissed her in the street outside the restaurant.

'How was your flight up from Melbourne?' she said.

'On time and comfortable. I can't ask for more.'

'It…it's nice to see you again,' she said. 'I'm sorry Daisy can't be here. She'll be upset she missed you, her favourite male human, or…or she would be if she were human and she knew about it, but of course she's not.' Well, that was a great start, mumbling inanely about her dog.

'I'm upset I missed her,' he said gallantly. 'Where is she today?'

'I like this café but they don't welcome dogs, so I left her at work.' She waved her hand to indicate her shop front, diagonally across the road. 'We're over there.'

'I walked past your building on my way here from the hotel. It's very smart and with great street presence.'

'Yes, we get passing trade as well as clients who know us by reputation,' she said, knowing her voice sounded stilted. Where was that easy flow of conversation from their dinner last Saturday?

Trouble was, she couldn't stop worrying about what might be going on there over the road and it was strangling her thoughts. She should be there, not having lunch with someone. But she was here, and she wanted to enjoy the rare treat of being with a man as attractive as Josh.

'We should order,' she said. 'The food is excellent here.'

She handed Josh a menu. In doing so she knocked over the open bottle of sparkling mineral water Mara had brought to the table. Water spilled, fizzing, all over the table. She swore under her breath, the same word several times, as she tried to mop up the water with the paper napkins from the table. 'I'm sorry, so sorry. First my dog muddies your trousers and now I've spilled water all over you.' She was conscious of her voice rising. She took a deep breath to bring it back down.

'No need to apologise. There's no water on me.'

'Really?'

He grabbed some napkins and mopped up the water that had formed a puddle on his side of the table. 'There, all gone.'

'I'm sorry, I really am,' she said, feeling wretched.

'You've already said sorry twice, no need for a third. You've got nothing to apologise for.'

'So long as you're not drenched.'

'I'm perfectly dry,' he said.

'You're sure?'

'I'm absolutely sure.' His smile was kind and reassuring. It made her want to sob. *Pull yourself together, Eloise.*

'Good,' she said. 'I'll order another bottle of water when we order our meal.'

'Problem solved.'

She attempted a smile. 'Shall I try again?' Very carefully, she passed him the menu, which he took from her with exaggerated care and made her laugh.

'What do you recommend?' he asked.

'Anything I've tried on the menu is very good. It's simple café food but very well prepared. I… I'm not very hungry so I'll order a quinoa and hummus salad.'

'I'll try the salmon,' he said.

'Good choice,' she said.

He leaned towards her. 'Before we order I want to make it clear lunch is my treat.'

'Oh, but—'

'No buts. I invited you, I pay.'

She knew she would sound ungracious if she argued. 'Thank you.'

Mara came to take their orders, bringing with her a pile of new napkins. Josh asked her to bring more water, Eloise for her favourite white wine.

Josh waited for the waitress to be out of earshot. 'Are you okay? You don't seem yourself. Or at least not the you I know from our last two meetings.'

'Absolutely fine,' she said but to her horror her voice wobbled and she had to sniff back a sudden, threatening tear.

'Are you sure? You seem a little stressed.' His voice was calm and soothing.

'*Stressed?* Yes. I am a little stressed.' She paused. 'Something horrible has happened and I wasn't going to tell you and now I guess I should or you'll wonder why I'm all over the place.'

'I'm listening,' he said.

Eloise realised what a relief it would be to share the awfulness of the threat she was under. Her staff were too invested in the business to give an impartial opinion, although she was pleased at how they had banded around her with wholehearted support. Josh was a tech mogul. Maybe he would have some advice on how to shut her problem down.

The wine had arrived. Josh poured two glasses. As he reached across the table to hand it to her she became intensely aware of the fresh male scent of him. Whatever aftershave or cologne he wore, it made her want to swoon. When she got to know him better— if that ever happened—she'd ask him what brand it was.

She took a good slug of wine and put her

glass back on the table, leaned across to him and lowered her voice. 'I've run foul of one of the local social media fashion influencers—an eastern suburbs woman who goes by the handle @*lindytheblonde*. She has more than two million followers and has threatened to ruin me. Soon, she told me, no bride will want to wear an Eloise Evans Atelier gown at her wedding.'

Josh frowned. 'That doesn't sound good.'

'It's not good. I know this woman. I've dressed her as a bridesmaid three times. She wasn't easy to deal with then. Now she's finally a bride, she's morphed into a fully-fledged Bridezilla.' She was aware her voice rose on the last words and forced herself to lower it.

'How did the threat come about?'

'The first conflict came when I wouldn't let her jump the waiting list. I got the "Do you know who I am?" thing then. I knew perfectly well who she was and, to be honest, wished she'd go somewhere else for her gown. After some huffing and puffing she had to wait for her name to come to the top like everyone else.'

'Your waiting list is a clever strategy. I suspect it makes people value your product.'

She smiled a shaky smile. 'It's quite deliberate. Exclusivity is our selling point.'

'And people are prepared to pay for it.'

'Yes,' she said. 'But not @*lindytheblonde*.'

Eloise looked around the café, just in case, but it was still early for lunch and the tables nearest to them were empty. Only a few people walked by on the street. She lowered her voice to practically a murmur. She and Josh had to have their heads almost touching for him to hear her.

'She came for her first consultation yesterday afternoon. She wanted a very extravagant, very expensive gown and was furious I wouldn't give it to her gratis in return for a social media tag. She expects everything for free and I don't give freebies. They devalue my brand. I have a marketing strategy that includes paid advertising and placements. I'm grateful to bloggers and social media—brides sharing their wedding dresses on their pages helped grow my business immensely in the early days—but I keep advertising and editorial separate. I didn't get the chance to tell her I would consider advertising in her space as she has such big numbers.'

'She wasn't happy?'

'She was outraged. She flounced out of my

workroom telling me in no uncertain terms where I could stick my wedding dresses.'

'Not a nice lady.'

'Indeed not.'

'Good riddance to bad rubbish, I would say.'

'That's what I thought. Until she started a smear campaign against me. It's all over social media. She must have gone straight home and started posting—and you know how quickly gossip spreads on the internet.'

'What dirt could she find to smear you with?'

'Dirt? I hope I haven't got any dirt to find. But she's outing me as the wedding dress designer who never wants a wedding of her own. "Would you trust your dream dress with a woman who scorns your dreams? How can a designer who has sworn off marriage possibly understand the needs of a bride?" That kind of thing.' She shuddered. 'She's given me some horrible hashtags.'

Josh's eyebrows rose. 'Is that true? That you don't ever want to get married?'

'She's twisted my words somewhat but it's mostly true.' She shrugged. 'I've made no secret of it. Now I wish I'd kept my mouth shut about my views.'

'Why such a strong opinion?'

'To close down well-meaning people, basically. I broke off a long-term relationship more than a year ago. I nearly got engaged, but realised in time that he was totally and utterly Mr Wrong for me. I do *not* want to rush into another serious relationship.' She'd lost herself in trying to be what Craig had wanted her to be.

'I get that,' Josh said. She thought about the 'most eligible bachelor' lists he'd appeared on and thought he might have his own story to tell about relationships gone wrong.

'But the thing with brides is that they're in their own little bubble of couple love and they want you to be floating up there alongside them. Nearly every consultation, every fitting, sooner or later out it comes: "When will you be making your own dream dress, Eloise?" I found the easiest reply was to tell them I hadn't found the right man yet. That soon proved to be totally the wrong reply.'

'Why?'

'Because it inspired them with zeal to find me the right man. Their lonely brother/cousin/ friend/bitter divorced uncle or even gay guy friend they were convinced hadn't met the right woman.' She made pretend tearing-out-her-hair motions. 'Aaargh! I didn't want to meet them, and they most likely didn't want to meet me. It became so much easier to say I didn't ever want to get married. I didn't think it would backfire on me like this.'

'You really meant it? About not wanting to get married?'

'Never say never. But it's true for me right now. I can't see a wedding on the horizon for me for a long time.'

'I get that,' he said.

'Working in the wedding dress business, I deal with some deliriously happy couples. Their glow can't help but wear off on you, like glitter. I sometimes envy them. But you can really get to see the underbelly of romance too. I'd never name names, but it's got so I can predict which of my brides' weddings won't last a year. It's made me realise too many people get married for the wrong reasons.'

He frowned. 'What are the right reasons?'

'Being darn sure you're compatible for one thing. I value my independence and I don't want to give over any part of my life for someone else to control. So yes, @lindytheblonde is partly right about me but she's very wrong that I'm not the right person to help another woman's wedding dreams come true. I think

I've proved that and I can't bear that her vindictiveness might affect my business.'

'Has it affected your business?'

'Sadly, yes. Three names came off the waiting list within minutes of her first posting. Heaven knows what carnage is to come.'

'What do you intend to do? Take legal action?'

'I can see Mara heading our way with food. How about we talk about my options over lunch?' Eloise suggested. She felt so much better for having unburdened herself.

Today Eloise looked vintage sexy in a tight, red and white polka-dotted pencil skirt, a wide belt and a white knit top that looked fabulous with her wavy black hair and bold red lipstick. So very, very different from anything Tori would ever wear. The top was finished with a wide, loose bow that drew attention to the subtle cleavage on display. However, he doubted she wore it to purposely tease and entice. Those were the clothes she wore to work, she'd come straight from her premises across the road to this café. She was a fashion designer, she had a 'look' and it suited her natural sensuality superbly. Josh couldn't keep his eyes off her.

He was more and more intrigued by Eloise. He didn't think he'd ever met a beautiful young woman with an anti-marriage stance. Guys, yes. Including himself. He wasn't a huge fan of weddings either.

There weren't enough good marriages in his family to make him aspire to the matrimonial state. His brother was a bully and on to his second wife. His mother, so she'd explained to him, had been lonely and unhappy in her marriage to his ex-father, hence the affair with her tennis coach. And yet, when Josh was eighteen years old, graduated from high school and already earning his own living, she had informed him she was going back to the man who had kicked them out. More for the affluent lifestyle she'd been used to and had sorely missed than anything to do with love, she had admitted. She hated living in the North End.

But there was a proviso—Josh himself wasn't to darken the door. His mother had to meet him off the premises. The unexpected betrayal had been a painful blow—he had still needed her. How could she accept separation from him in return for financial comfort?

Thankfully his aunt had stepped up to assure him he would always have a home in the North End. The security of Aunt Lil's love had done much to soothe the sting of his mother's betrayal. Now he was able to ensure his aunt was secure financially for the rest of her days.

Yet, to his mother's credit, she had worked to keep up her relationship with him, just as she had with her older son when he'd been forbidden to her. In recent years, he had tentatively rebuilt his relationship with his mother. Not to what it had been when it had been him and her against his father and his world, but something both of them were moderately happy with. However, he had never trusted her enough to confide in her about his vendetta against his ex-father. She was too beholden to him to be trusted.

Control. Eloise was right in her thinking. In that marriage his mother had ceded all independence to her husband's control. But surely men of his generation didn't behave like that with their wives? Even with his insistence that all dating was casual, he'd been stung by women impressed by his wealth, who saw him as a potential meal ticket. But to him a relationship had to be one of equals— his mother had been trapped in an unhappy marriage, as she'd given up her career to support her husband's and been financially unable to support her sons.

The waitress winked at him when she put his plate in front of him, not so Eloise could see. He couldn't tell Eloise but during his first days in Sydney he had spent quite some time in this café, watching her atelier in the hope of seeing her going in or coming out. This waitress had asked him if he was waiting for his fiancée to have a fitting at the exclusive bridal store over the road. He'd made a noncommittal answer she had obviously misinterpreted. Did she think Eloise was his fiancée? From the knowing way she looked from him to Eloise he believed so—and that she approved of their 'romance'. He swallowed a curse. How would he ever explain that to Eloise if the girl said anything about his prior visit to her café?

He was glad for the diversion of eating their meals. He didn't want to talk about weddings or anything related to them. But suddenly he didn't feel very hungry.

'Are you going to finish your salmon?' Eloise asked.

He noticed she'd barely touched her salad. 'No. If you'd like—'

She smiled. 'Not for me. But Daisy is very

fond of salmon. If you don't want it, I could take a doggy bag back to her.'

'She'd be very welcome.'

'My mother will be picking her up soon to take her home with her. I asked her to mind Daisy for me, as I've been invited to a big pull-out-all-the-stops wedding out in the country this weekend.'

'It's convenient your mother could look after her for you.'

'Yes. Only it might be for nothing. I'm not sure I can bear to go to the wedding. Horrid *@lindytheblonde* is going to be there and I don't think I can face her.'

'That doesn't sound like you.' He corrected himself. 'The you that I've got to know, that is. Wouldn't she see it as a victory if you didn't go?'

'Probably. And Becca, the bride, might be disappointed if I cry off. We've become good friends. I dressed her for her first wedding and this is her second.'

'Do you often get repeat business?'

'Quite often. In this case she's got it right the second time. Husband number two, Simon, is a fabulous guy. I'd like to be there to celebrate with her. There's also the fact that among all those guests might be potential clients. But I really don't think I can face @ *lindytheblonde*.' Her voice hitched. 'My presence will only point out the truth of what she's saying about me because I don't have a plus-one to take to the wedding.'

'I can be your plus-one.' The words slipped out as if of their own volition.

Her eyes widened. 'You could? But you're going back to Boston.'

'I don't have to. I'm my own boss.'

'Really? You'd really do that for me?'

'It would hardly be a hardship,' he said drily.

'It's out near Bowral, south west of Sydney, very posh. The wedding is to be held in a grand country house owned by the groom's family. I've been invited to stay the night. We made the bride's gown and the attendants'. It will be a beautiful wedding. But it does mean a nearly two-hour drive out there and then back the next day. If you're sure you can spare the time…?'

'I can do that,' he said. He didn't like seeing her being ill-treated by the woman.

'Thank you! I accept your offer.' She clapped her hands together in delight, her cheeks flushed. She leaned over and kissed him on the mouth. 'Have you got a tux with you?'

'No, I didn't see the need.'

'No matter. We can tailor one for you. We sometimes do that for special grooms. Actually, there are some brides who like a white tux as well. We have an excellent tailor on the staff. You'd just have to come in for a fitting. Now. After lunch. I'll take your measurements myself. Then another fitting tomorrow.'

Josh gulped at the prospect of Eloise taking his inside leg measurement. 'Great,' he choked out. What the hell was he letting himself in for?

CHAPTER SIX

THERE WASN'T TIME to waste. As soon as they
finished lunch, Eloise ushered Josh over the
road and through the door to Eloise Evans
Atelier. She gave him a quick tour around
the ground-floor salon. As she did, she immediately felt her tension ratchet down a
notch. Her business was everything to her.
She would defend it in any legal way she
could. Josh had offered her a lifeline as her
plus-one for the weekend wedding. With
him by her side, she could hold her head up
high against any barbs from that malicious
influencer.

The spacious room proudly celebrated
femininity. One of her clients had called it
a shrine to brides and maybe that wasn't far
off. The space was decorated in shades of
white and cream, with plush carpets under-
foot and silver vases filled with magnifi-

cent fresh flower arrangements strategically placed. Bolts of the finest fabrics sourced from all around the world spilled out of a large, open armoire she'd imported from France and shimmered under the light of a lavish antique crystal chandelier.

'We pride ourselves on luxury and exclusivity,' she explained. 'The salon is set up to see one bridal party at a time—the bride, her attendants, her mother, whoever she chooses to bring with her. Appointments are timed so that brides are unlikely to bump into other brides.'

'And the price reflects the level of service,' he said. She liked the way he took her 'girly' business so seriously and seemed to have an innate understanding of how she operated.

'And comfort,' she said. Upholstered chairs were strategically placed around the space. Champagne was chilling in a silver ice bucket, canapés would be offered. And tissues for the tears of those brides overcome by the beauty of their gowns and their mothers overcome by the beauty of their daughters.

All that was missing was a bride trying on a gown from the rack filled with garments in various shades of pale to see which shapes best suited her and twirling in front of the large mirrors with ornate gilt frames. A girl from a very wealthy northern suburbs family should have been doing just that right now. Only she'd cancelled at the last minute, citing 'philosophical differences with the designer' as her reason. Even the thought of it made Eloise grit her teeth.

Josh's expression was vaguely hunted, his eyes glazed as he looked around. 'Impressive,' he said.

'I wanted to recreate the kind of elegant salon that impressed me when I worked in Paris. Getting fitted for a wedding dress should be a memorable, happy experience and a real treat.'

'I'm sure it is,' he said. 'But—'

'There's a *but*?'

He shuddered. 'I feel totally out of place here. I'm too tall, too big, too *male*.'

He was all that without a doubt. *Oh, yes.* And so very handsome. She couldn't be happier that he had offered to escort her to Becca's wedding. He was perfect. And if *@lindytheblonde* got wind that he was a billionaire, that would be even better.

She laughed. 'Men aren't usually part of the wedding dress decision. Remember, it's thought to be bad luck for a groom to see the bride's dress before their wedding. Old traditions die hard. I think you'll be more comfortable in the workroom upstairs.'

'Perhaps I could go out and buy a tuxedo rather than you make—'

She shook her head. 'Not happening. The least I can do for you in return for accompanying me to the wedding is to provide a bespoke tuxedo. You're used to having your clothes made bespoke, I can tell.'

'I go to the best tailor in Boston.'

'Besides, I couldn't possibly have my plus-one accompany me in anything that wasn't classy and impeccably tailored.'

He looked at her, bemused. 'I'm uncertain if you're joking or not.'

'Mostly not joking. I'm judged by the quality of my clothes. I guess I'll be judged by the quality of your suit if @*lindytheblonde* really has the daggers out for me at the wedding. I don't want you caught up in it.'

Eloise led Josh up the stairs, and through another set of doors to the workroom.

'This is the heart of my business,' she said proudly. 'Where a bride's dreams of the perfect dress become reality.'

This large room was a constant hub of activity. Her team of seamstresses sat at industrial sewing machines or hand-stitching garments, mostly white, some the myriad colours of bridesmaids' dresses. They all wore gloves to protect the very expensive fabrics.

Trolleys were hung with clipped-together bunches of brown paper pattern pieces. Dressmaker's dummies were draped with pinned and half-finished gowns. Various samples of lace and trims and ribbons dangled from metal racks. A mood board for a large upcoming wedding where they were dressing not just the bride and her attendants but also all the female members of their extended families dominated one corner.

Eloise breathed in the scent of freshly cut fabrics, of paper and sewing machines. She loved it all. Most nights it was a wrench to go home. She couldn't bear it being under threat.

She stood at the front of the room and addressed her team. 'I'd like to introduce you all to Josh Taylor. He's accompanying me to the Sanderson wedding and we need to get him into a tux, pronto. We'll need to pull out all the stops.'

She was surprised at the wave of giggles that rippled through the room. Her close friend and second in command, Vinh Tran, came over to her, unable to suppress an enormous smile. 'Hi, Josh; we were wondering when Eloise was going to introduce you to us,' she said, for the room's benefit.

'What?' The word exploded from Eloise.

She looked anxiously up at Josh. Surely he wouldn't think she'd boasted to her friends and colleagues about their date, blown it up to something so much more than it was? He shifted from one foot to the other, looking as uncomfortable as she was feeling.

She'd told Vinh she was going on her first date in for ever with a visiting American when they'd been working on the pink tea dress she'd worn that night, but that was as far as it had gone.

'You mean you haven't seen it?' said Vinh.

'Seen what? I don't know what you're talking about.'

Vinh brought over her tablet and, without a word, enlarged the images on screen to show her.

Eloise's hand shot to her mouth to stifle her gasp. There she was in close-up, in her red spotted skirt, leaning across the table in the nearby café and kissing Josh. It had only been a brief kiss, but the camera gave it so much more significance. There was another of them talking, their heads so close they were almost touching, smiling into each other's eyes. The images were close, intimate, and she was glowing. *They looked so good together.*

'Where did these come from?'

'They were posted on one of the local gossip sites.' Vinh read out the caption. '"*New man for celebrity frock queen?*" I must say you look gorgeous. And…er…so do you, Josh.'

Vinh, a petite Vietnamese Australian, had been friends with Eloise since the first days of their fashion design degree. Eloise had dropped out soon after her internship in Paris ended, as she figured she'd learned enough about the nuts and bolts of design and patternmaking and had keenly observed how the French bridal couture house had operated. Vinh had completed her degree and, while she was an excellent designer, she was also interested in the business side of running a label. But Vinh hadn't wanted to start her own. Each of the friends had not had good experiences working for established fashion companies.

Eloise had set up by herself on a small scale, working from an industrial site in Alexandria.

Some of those girls for whom she'd made prom dresses had asked if she could work her magic on their wedding dresses. Word-of-mouth recommendations and exposure on social media had given her the bookings and the confidence to expand into Double Bay, or Double Pay as it was colloquially known. Two years ago she'd asked Vinh to join her in the business. It had proved to be an excellent decision.

Now Vinh was obviously taken with Josh and kept giving Eloise meaningful sideways glances of approval. Dear heaven, please don't let Josh notice, Eloise prayed.

Eloise frowned. 'But who—?'

'The waitress?' Josh said.

'Mara? Maybe.'

'A lot of people walk past there—it could have been anyone with a camera phone who recognised you,' said Vinh.

Josh turned to Eloise. 'Isn't this good publicity for you? It takes the sting out of the attack from the influencer.' He paused. 'And I agree, you look beautiful.'

A soft, collective sigh sounded through the room. Eloise felt the sudden sting of tears and blinked down hard on them. She was as susceptible to romance as anyone else—more so perhaps, given her profession—it was just she fought so hard against it for herself. She couldn't let herself get to like Josh too much. He'd soon be winging his way back home. There would be no chance to see if the attraction between them could lead to anything deeper.

'In fact, it's very romantic,' said Vinh. 'And if you're going to that big wedding together on the weekend, that's all the better.'

Vinh and the rest of the team were aware of her anguish over the influencer's damaging posts. And the fact if the business slid downhill their jobs could be at risk.

Eloise looked at the photo again. She'd like a copy for herself but didn't dare admit it. Later, she'd take a screen shot. 'You're both right,' she said.

'Let's hope it goes viral, then,' said Vinh. She turned to Eloise. 'Before I forget, your mum popped in to pick up Daisy. She said she was double parked and couldn't wait for you.'

'Thanks,' said Eloise, disappointed she wouldn't see her little foster dog until after the weekend. People sometimes asked her how she liked living alone. She would reply she was never alone, as she had a series of canine companions. When it came to love, dogs were so much more reliable than humans.

Josh seemed genuinely disappointed too. 'I'm sorry I won't see Daisy.'

Vinh then turned to Josh. 'We need to take your measurements for that rush order tux.'

Eloise caught Josh's eye. For a moment she was tempted to take the tailor's tape measure and do it herself, as she'd suggested at the café. But she couldn't bring herself to do it. There was a lot of body measuring involved for a bespoke suit so it would fit and drape perfectly. She just couldn't. It would be somehow too…intimate. She was too aware of him, of the feelings aroused by that kiss, to trust herself.

'Yes,' she said to Vinh. 'Can you please handle him…er… I mean, handle that? You know what I mean.' Her friend laughed. Josh looked discomfited in a way she found very appealing.

'I think the Italian wool and silk fabric in midnight-blue,' she said. 'What do you think, Josh?'

He shrugged. 'I'll put myself in your expert hands.' Eloise blushed high on her cheekbones and hoped he didn't notice. *She'd like that very much.*

* * *

During the process of being measured for his tux, Josh became aware of how liked and admired Eloise was by her staff. How hard she worked. What a fair manager she was. How very unfair it was that the spiteful actions of a disgruntled Bridezilla should threaten the business she loved so passionately.

If he were Eloise, he would be immediately seeking a way to ruin that influencer. He was vengeful and didn't mind admitting it. Long after his opponent had forgotten about his attack on Josh or one of his enterprises—or thought they'd got away with it—he would strike. *The smiling assassin*, one of his business associates had labelled him. And they hadn't meant it as a compliment.

He hadn't always been that hard, vengeful person. As a kid, he'd been sunny, good-natured, secure in his family and status. All that had changed the day he'd been evicted from his home and the life he'd thought was his by birth. Then he'd had to use his smarts and any weapon available to him to forge ahead. He treated people with honesty, and if he didn't get it in return then they would get their comeuppance. He knew he would never get the revenge he wanted against the man who had raised him—his ex-father's fortune was too blue-chip, too established—but he could certainly chip away at the edges of it. And, oh, how he would gloat to see him up before the bankruptcy court.

He was glad he was able to help Eloise by accompanying her to the wedding as her plus-one. How wise an action that was for him, he hadn't paused to think. Or how he would explain it to Tori. Eloise needed help, and on impulse he'd come to the rescue. Now he realised there was yet another way he could help her get revenge on her opponent.

He waited until he'd been measured, every bit as skilfully and thoroughly as by his gentleman's tailor in Boston, and been asked to return later in the afternoon for his first fitting. There would be two more the next morning.

Eloise escorted him downstairs. She paused at the entrance to the citadel of girliness. 'We'll see you in two hours. I've got half the team working on your tux.' She looked up at him, her blue eyes warm and sincere, fringed with those outrageously fake black lashes that were fun and glamorous on her but he'd think over-the-top on anyone else. 'Thank you again, Josh. The paparazzi actually played right into our hands. Hopefully there'll be some buzz ahead of us by the time we go to the wedding together on Saturday.'

He lowered his voice to be heard only by her. 'I've thought of a way to get even more buzz and to knock the wind right out of your detractor's sails.'

Her brow pleated into a frown. 'And that would be?'

'What if I pretended to be your fiancé for the weekend?'

Her eyes widened. 'You…you'd be my fake fiancé?'

'In terms of business strategy, it's an excellent idea. If you turn up to the wedding with a fiancé on your arm, it negates everything the influencer says about your attitude to marriage.'

'That's true.' She paused. 'It's drastic though, isn't it? I'd have to give the idea some thought.'

He had a sudden inspiration. 'It would help me out too. Lately I've been put on a number of ludicrous "most eligible bachelors" lists and that really bugs me. Gossip of an engagement will put those lists immediately out of date.'

'So it could work for both of us,' she said slowly.

'It could,' he said.

She looked up at him. 'Okay. Let's do it.' Although her words were bold, the accompanying smile was a tad shaky.

'Then, after the wedding, you can take your real revenge.'

'What do you mean?' she said.

'This is how I would handle it if she were my opponent. You will already have weakened her by showing she was wrong about you not wanting to marry. Next, I would get my business analysts to go through her site looking for any inconsistencies and weaknesses in her enterprises. Presumably, she gets her income from advertisers who pay her for her endorsements of their products. I would look for even the slightest instance where she might have crossed the line that I could use against her. Then I would use my muscle to ensure the advertisers did not see her as being the best spokesperson or brand for their products any longer. Ultimately I would bring her down. As she intended to bring you down.'

Her eyes widened. 'That's really ruthless. And not very ethical.'

He shrugged. 'That's how the world works.' He'd learned from the best when it came to stone-hearted ruthlessness: his ex-father.

Eloise stayed silent for a long moment and he could see by the expressions flashing across her face that she was reassessing her opinion of him. And it was definitely downward. For the best, perhaps. He didn't want her building any expectations of him.

Finally she spoke. 'I don't know that I would want to go that far, regardless of what you might do in the same situation. However, the fake fiancé idea is a good one, if we can carry it off.'

'You'll have to guide me there. I know nothing about being engaged.'

'I would have to have a doting fiancé on my arm. What I mean is, we'll have to make it look believable. You know, that we…er… were actually in love with each other.'

'That's a point,' he said. 'We might get our first chance now. Don't turn around, but your friend Vinh is peeking around the door upstairs.'

Eloise smiled. 'Is she, now? Let's start how we mean to continue. Give her something to take back to the workroom, and get the gossip started, shall we?' She wound her arms around his neck and kissed him, her mouth sweet and warm under his.

Almost immediately Josh forgot that the kiss was staged as he pulled her close and kissed her back.

CHAPTER SEVEN

BY EARLY FRIDAY afternoon Josh's tuxedo was fitted and finished, the trouser hems breaking perfectly on the new dress shoes he'd bought the day before at a Double Bay boutique. The jacket had a whimsical blue-and-white-spotted silk lining, which had been a surprise to him.

'If I'd known you a little better I could have fitted the design to your interests, even had the lining custom-printed if there'd been time,' Eloise murmured so no one else could hear. 'After all, tuxedos can be a tad on the stuffy side for a young guy.'

He stood in his new tux at the front of the workroom for a final check. Eloise and her delightful friend Vinh then circled him, while he stood there captive in his new suit. The two women snipped loose threads, tucked, pulled, and prodded the fabric into place, laughing as they did so until it dawned on him they were making a game of it. Finally, laughing himself, he told them to cease and desist. Eloise's touch, no matter how light and playful, was altogether too distracting. Again he wondered what he might have unwittingly got himself into.

She looked sexy as hell in citrus-yellow hip-hugging retro-style cut-off trousers and a short swing top that gave a tantalising hint of the creamy skin of her waist when she turned. High heels gave her a delightful wiggle when she walked. She wore her clothes like a theatrical costume, he realised. Did she hide her real self behind the drama of vintage style? Or was the dressing up just part of her creative nature? It was no matter. It was fun. *She was fun.* He couldn't remember when he'd last felt more relaxed.

Again he thought how much Tori would like Eloise. He wished Tori would contact her twin soon. The longer Tori left it, the deeper Josh got into this friendship with Eloise—which was more than a friendship but less than a relationship or even an affair—the more difficult it would be to explain his role in their reunion when it ultimately all came out.

In the interests of transparency, he had

called Tori that morning, Sydney time, to tell her his business dealings had taken him back to Sydney. It was stretching the truth somewhat, as, while he had actually made business appointments, the primary purpose had been that inexplicable and compelling urge to see Eloise again.

He'd told Tori about the lunch. Then casually mentioned he was acting as plus-one for a wedding on the upcoming weekend.

Immediately Tori had pounced. 'Are you sure you're not getting in a little too deep, Josh? I asked you to get a close look at her. Not to get close *to* her.' She'd paused. 'You're not developing a thing for her, are you?'

'Of course not,' he'd denied, knowing he was blustering, knowing he was not quite telling the entire truth.

Whatever Tori defined as a *thing*, he wasn't feeling it for Eloise. He found her undeniably hot, beautiful, smart. He liked her. She made him laugh, loosened him up, made him relax. Inspired him to do crazy things like pretend to be her fiancé to help her vanquish a business threat. But it wasn't a *thing*. He wasn't falling for her, definitely not. Tori needed to be absolutely clear about that.

So did he.

Now Eloise pulled him aside so they could speak without being overhead. 'Are you free for practice after work tonight?'

'Practice?'

'Fiancé practice.'

His thoughts ran in one rather exciting direction but he suspected she didn't mean that. 'Run that by me again?'

'We're meant to be an engaged couple and we have to be convincing at the wedding. That influencer woman will pick a phony couple a mile off. We have to seem genuine. That means we have to get our stories straight—you know, how we met, how long we've been together, that kind of stuff.'

'I didn't realise it would involve all that.'

'I didn't either until I started to think about it. I've never been a fake fiancée before. Or any kind of fiancée actually. Do you want to back out? You can at any time, you know. I won't hold you to it.'

'No, not at all. I gave my word.' He frowned. 'But I didn't realise it would involve so much lying.'

'Might be wise not to think of it as lying. Rather…' She thought about it for a moment 'Not a lie as such, but rather a targeted business strategy of purposeful evasion.'

He laughed. 'Where did you get that from?'

'I did a business course when I knew I'd be setting up on my own,' she said. 'I can talk the talk when I need to.'

'Well, I guess that's something I should know about you. There must be more.'

'Exactly. That's why we need to practise our stories.'

'Okay. Count me in.'

'Why don't I pop round to your hotel after I finish work? It's only around the corner. We could maybe get a pizza or something.' She put up her hand. 'No. Wait. As my fiancé, you would be expected to be familiar with my apartment. Do you mind coming round to mine? I'll give you the address.'

'Sure.'

'In the meantime, you think of a few questions to ask me, and I'll think of a few questions to ask you. I'll pick up some Thai take-out on my way home.'

Eloise was only too aware that Josh, charming as he might appear, was a tough, driven businessman. No one got to be a billionaire before the age of thirty without a finely honed edge of ruthlessness. His comments on her business revealed a shrewd eye for potential profit. That was verified in the many news and finance pages she'd delved into online to find out more about him.

Yet his revenge strategy for @lindytheblonde had shocked her. His eyes had narrowed and his face set hard as he'd outlined his plan. His fluency made her think he had exacted such a revenge before against someone who had crossed him. Perhaps more than one opponent. She realised she would have to keep her wits about her in any dealings with him. Who knew how ruthless he might be towards people in his personal life?

And yet she'd seen a different side to billionaire Josh. A man kind to a scruffy little dog. A man with a sense of humour who had completely won over her fiercely protective best friend, Vinh—not to mention everyone else in the atelier. Then there was the man who'd offered that whacky solution to her problem with @lindytheblonde. She considered herself to be a creative thinker but a fake engagement wouldn't have crossed her mind in a million years.

Accepting his off-the-wall offer had kicked her relationship with Josh up to a different level that taking him as a plus-one to the wedding would not have. He was no longer a stranger, yet not quite a friend—she was way too attracted to him to put him in the friend category. She didn't have lustful thoughts as she did for Josh with her male friends. Yet their situations meant he couldn't be a potential boyfriend either.

They were co-conspirators in a fake engagement and that would involve a disconcerting level of fake intimacy. But it really was a good idea. If only she—they—could carry it off. Because if they didn't, if she and Josh were revealed as frauds, she'd be a laughing stock. And what that meant for her business could only be bad.

Now she sat opposite Josh, the coffee table between them, each on one of the two squashy cream sofas that formed the focal point of her living room. A half-empty bottle of white wine and their two glasses sat on the coffee table.

She'd inherited this spacious nineteen-thirties apartment from her grandmother—the same one who had taught her to sew—and it was her haven. That grandmother had loved her unconditionally, and had helped her understand the reasons her mother had kept her adoption from her. Still, she'd never been quite able to shake off the knowledge that her grandmother had known and been part of the conspiracy. Even someone as close and doting as her grandmother had lied to her.

She knew how fortunate she was; the price of real estate in this suburb was astronomical. In fact, Double Bay was the wealthiest area in the state with this adjoining area coming in second. The bow-fronted windows looked out over Rushcutters Bay Park and beyond to the waters of the harbour. She could actually see the spot where Daisy had so fortuitously redirected her ball to Josh.

Josh had changed into black jeans and a black cashmere sweater. He looked comfortable, relaxed and super-hot. Not only was he handsome, but he also exuded a male virility that she could not help but respond to with thoughts bordering on the sinful. She wouldn't have any trouble pretending to be attracted to him as his fake fiancée. Keeping her hands off him might be the problem.

They'd chatted generalities as they'd polished off the Thai dinner but, the meal cleared, it was time to get down to the business of prepping themselves to be a believable couple.

'Okay, let's start our preparation for operation fake engagement,' she said. 'Have you ever done any acting? Theatre? Drama studies at school?'

'No.' His expression told her he found the very idea disdainful.

'Me neither,' she said. 'I freeze with nerves the second anyone so much points me in the direction of a stage.'

'I find that hard to believe,' he said. 'You seem so confident.'

'On a one-to-one level maybe,' she said. 'But that does nothing for me when stage fright hits. So when it comes to playing our roles as an engaged couple, we're going to have to wing it.'

'Improvisation is what they call it,' he said.

She nodded. 'We have to think about what a real engaged couple would do and then improvise accordingly. Heaven knows I see enough of them around me.'

'My friends are starting to succumb to the lure of matrimony, so I know a few,' he said. He said *succumb* as if they were being felled by some noxious disease. With her own opinions on marriage being blasted all over the internet, she could hardly be critical of his.

'They're super-sweet to each other,' she said. 'Most have cutesie pet names.'

Josh shuddered. 'Can we please not go there?'

'I agree. I don't think I could do the pet names with a straight face. But some of my close friends call me Ellie. I won't mind if you drop the occasional "Ellie" in the interests of authenticity.'

'"Ellie". I like that. It suits you. But please, don't even think of calling me "Joshy".' The pained expression on his face made her laugh.

'Okay, no calling you J— No, I can't even say it in jest.'

She paused, not sure how to bring up the next subject. 'Engaged couples are usually very affectionate towards each other. Physically affectionate, I mean. Dropping little kisses on their beloved, lots of snuggling and smooching. You know.'

He looked at her for a long moment, and again she had that heady sense of connection. She realised she was leaning towards him, as if straining to be in his arms, and he was leaning towards her. He cleared his throat. 'I don't think we'll have any trouble doing that,' he said.

She sat back on her sofa. 'Me neither. In fact I… I…well, I think we—that is to say I—might have the opposite problem. Being too enthusiastic perhaps.'

'Yes,' he said slowly.

'So only public displays of affection. We need to turn down the dial in private. It's not that I don't trust myself... Well, it is, actually. But we've agreed that neither of us is ready for a relationship and I don't want—'

'I know,' he said hoarsely.

'So that's agreed?'

He nodded. 'Hands off in private.'

Eloise tucked her feet up under her on the sofa. She'd changed into skinny, cuffed nineteen-fifties-style jeans and a red-and-white-checked shirt. 'I'm thinking of the questions people might ask us at the wedding.'

'You go first,' he said.

'Where did we meet?'

He indicated the front window with a wave. 'The dog park out there.'

'Correct. And that would mean we were presenting as an engaged couple just a week after we really did meet. Not very believable in my opinion.'

'You're right. This takes a bit of getting used to,' he said. 'Let me think. How about we first met in the US, say a few months ago?'

'Did you happen to be in Los Angeles at the time of Roxee's wedding?'

'So happens I did.'

'I was there too. Perhaps we met in LA. At a party. There were a number of parties leading up to the wedding.'

'To which, sadly, I was not invited,' he said with a mock-mournful expression.

'Shame. There was a party at a waterfront venue in Santa Monica. I went outside for a breath of fresh air. You were outside—'

'Taking a break from a particularly boring business dinner.' He paused. 'And I saw this dark-haired girl leaning against a palm tree. I was struck by her beauty.'

Eloise giggled. 'I like that. So what happened?

'I opened a conversation with a witty remark.'

'I responded with something equally witty.'

'We struck up a conversation. You hung on to my every word.'

'Huh! How about I made you laugh?'

'You do that in real life, so that could work. Then you said you had to get back to the party.'

'No! I'm sure I would have wanted to stay with you.'

'Would you?' he said.

'Yes.' Her gaze connected again with his in that surprisingly intimate way.

'Really?' he said, his voice husky.

'Really,' she said. Just as she had found an excuse to have coffee with him at the park. Deny it to herself all she liked, she'd been attracted to him from the start.

She snapped her eyes away. *This was just a game.* A game the success of which was important to her business, but a game just the same. She mustn't get carried away.

'So that's sorted.' She injected a no-nonsense briskness into her voice. 'What did you do next?'

'I got your number. And I called you straight away to check I'd got it right.'

'So when did you call me?'

'I asked you to call me when the party was finished. You did and we met up. Then I took you back to your hotel room.'

'And...?'

'We talked all night until the sun came up,' he said, a smile dancing around the corners of his sexy mouth. 'I was a gentleman.'

'And I was wishing you weren't.' She slapped her hand over her mouth. 'Scratch that!'

He laughed. 'But I wasn't such a gentleman the next night.'

'Really?' she said, trying to sound prim instead of turned on.

It took a real effort not to focus on imagining the exciting details of his fictional ungentlemanly behaviour and her fictional response. Since that first kiss she had spent too much time fantasising over the prospect of making love with Josh. Now he sat so near to her in the privacy of her home, it was impossible not to acknowledge that intense physical pull. 'And we spent as much time as we could together before you had to go back to Boston.'

'We did. In fact, we hardly left your hotel bedroom.' His tone was so exaggerated in its lasciviousness it made her laugh.

'If you say so,' she said.

'I wished so,' he said with a grin.

She was glad she had decided not to sit next to him on the sofa. It would be only too easy to let this game get out of hand and practise for real.

'Let's be serious,' she said. 'After the big celebrity wedding was over, I had to go to New York City to meet with one of Roxee's friends who'd just got engaged and wanted me to design her wedding gown. That part of the story is true.'

'So I flew to New York and we took up where we left off.'

'Don't say it, we hardly left the bedroom again and I saw nothing of New York.'

'Actually, this time you said it,' he said, laughter still warming his voice.

'Yes, I did,' she admitted. What a slip.

'You pick up the story now,' he said. 'What happened next?'

'I stayed in New York for as long as I could, but I had to get back to my work in Sydney. We said a sad goodbye.'

'We kept in touch via video chat.'

'And had lots of phone sex.' Again she clapped her hand to her mouth. 'I'm sorry— I don't know how that slipped out. Too much of that white wine you brought to go with the Thai food.' Was it wishful thinking that was causing her to blunder like this?

'I'm sure it would be the case if…if our story were true.' Was he humouring her? Or did he feel it too?

'We realised it was more than a fling,' she said.

'Then I flew over to Sydney last week to surprise you and propose.'

'And of course I was delighted.' She sat back in the sofa. 'That works for me. I think we've come up with a reasonable story. We just have to remember the details and stick with them.'

And not feel inexplicably sad because it sounded like a really romantic story and for a minute there she'd found herself wishing she were in it. On that beachfront at Santa Monica and falling in love with a stranger. Only the man in the story wasn't a stranger. It was Josh, real-life Josh, who was playing along with the game. And who looked so hot in those black jeans.

She untangled her legs, took a sip from her wine glass. 'Next question. Have you thought of anything you want to ask?'

He shook his head. 'I think you might know more about the subject of engagements than I do.'

'I know one question we're sure to be asked: *When is the wedding?* The second any-one gets engaged people start asking that.'

He frowned. 'That's got me stymied. To be honest, it's not something that has ever crossed my mind. What do you suggest?'

'We can't go wrong by saying spring. That gives us time to organise the hypothetical wedding. Say November, which is spring

Down Under. That's actually a lovely time to get married.'

'November it is,' he said. 'And the wedding is in Sydney not Boston?'

'Of course, as it's the bride's home town.' She had to say *the bride*. She simply couldn't bring herself to say *my*.

'Might they ask if you are intending to move to Boston after the wedding?' he said.

'Or if you intend to move to Sydney?'

They both fell silent. 'It's a tricky one,' she said finally. 'Why don't we say we're still fine-tuning the details?'

'Because actually Boston is your home town too,' he said slowly.

The silence that fell between them was more uncomfortable than the mock-marriage plans warranted. Finally Eloise broke it. 'So, moving on. The other question we're sure to be asked is *Can I see the engagement ring*?'

'I didn't think of that.' He swore under his breath. 'Will I have time to buy one in the morning before we leave for the wedding?'

'Thank you for the thought, but there's no need. I have a ring we can use. I inherited it from my grandmother. It's a gorgeous ruby and diamond ring. She called it a cocktail ring but it will suit our purpose. I've had the ring resized to fit me but never had a chance to wear it. Let me go and get it.'

Eloise got up from the sofa and went into the bedroom, glad of the excuse to escape from Josh for a moment and get back her equilibrium. She was shaking. This game was a dangerous one. She'd too easily become engrossed in the fiction of falling in love with Josh, a man who, the second the hypothetical scenario of their wedding came up, immediately assumed she'd be moving to Boston. It was only an off-the-cuff remark, meaningless in its context. But it underscored the reasons why no matter how much she enjoyed his company, no matter how much she fancied him, she could never allow herself to even think about falling for Josh in real life. He didn't appear to be controlling, but he certainly had a ruthless side to him. Who knew what he was really like?

With a bright smile pasted on her face, she came back into the living room to find Josh flicking through the glossy decorating magazine that had published a feature on her renovation of this apartment. He got up on her approach.

'Impressive what you've done here,' he said. 'The article says you could make your living in interior design if you changed your mind about wedding gowns.'

'Flattering, isn't it? But fashion is my first love, and I don't ever want to do anything else. Eloise Evans Atelier is more than just my work—it's my life. I enjoyed doing this place up but I wouldn't want to do it for a business. The apartment was my grandmother's and I wanted to honour all the lovely times I had with her here while at the same time updating her old-lady décor.'

'You've done a great job,' he said, looking around. 'It's very elegant.' She realised he must have seen the photos of her bedroom in the magazine and resisted the urge to show it to him.

She held up a small, rust-spotted box. 'But this ring I've left just as she had it because I value it that way. It's a large stone and I believe the setting was quite avant-garde for its time.'

'May I see it?' he said.

She flipped open the box and handed it to him. 'I don't know when it was last worn.'

One thing was for sure, her grandmother would not have approved of her intended subterfuge. And her mother would be horrified when she heard about it. But protecting her business was her priority—and she intended to do everything she could do to make @*lindytheblonde*'s attack on it fail.

Josh looked at the ring nestled in the very old velvet. 'I don't know anything about engagement rings but aren't they meant to be diamond? Will this be believable? I don't want to look cheap.' He was really entering into the spirit of the charade.

'I believe an engagement ring can be anything you want it to be. Anyone who knows anything about me knows I like vintage. I think this will pass muster. And it's actually very valuable.'

He held the little box awkwardly. 'Do…do I have to put it on your finger?'

She couldn't meet his eye. 'I… I think that would actually be a bit weird.' She took the ring from him and slipped it onto the third finger of her left hand. She held out her hand to display it, fingers splayed. 'This is how I'll show it off to anyone who asks. We don't need to give any details about where we got it or anything else.'

'It suits you,' he said. 'The ring suits you, your car suits you, so does the way you dress. You're your own woman. If people ask I'll say that's one of the reasons that attracted me to you.'

'Thank you,' she said, not sure what else to say, not sure if it was a compliment or not.

'It makes me wonder, do you actually need anyone else in your life?'

'I have friends, my mother—'

'I mean a life partner. Or are you like me, a lone wolf at heart?'

She looked up at him. 'I'm happy on my own but I… I don't think I'm a lone wolf. I've often felt there's something missing in my life, something intangible. Perhaps that's from being an only child. But as far as relationships go, I won't compromise and I've had bad luck with the wrong kind of man.'

A lazy smile hovered around the corners of his mouth. 'So, in fact, you haven't met "the right man" yet?'

She forced a laugh. 'Back to the old cliché. Perhaps in our role play at the wedding I can tell them I finally did meet him.'

She paused and the silence again became awkward. She had no experience to call upon to help her manage this situation. *A fake engagement.*

'I can't think of anything else we have to rehearse, can you?' she said.

She didn't give him a chance to reply. She really couldn't endure any more, alone here together in her apartment with all this make-believe talk of falling in love and phone sex and that undeniable, sizzling current of attraction between them.

'We'll have two hours in the car tomorrow to cover anything we've missed,' she said. 'The wedding starts at four. I need to be there around two as Becca, the bride, wants me to be there for a final check on her gown. I'd rather leave earlier than later. How about I pick you up from your hotel after breakfast?'

'Sounds like a plan to me,' he said.

She led him to the door. For a long moment they stood silently, facing each other. With her heels kicked off he seemed taller and she had to look a long way up. Finally, he put his hand to her face and traced a line to her cheek. Such a simple caress, yet it set her nerve ends tingling. 'I want to kiss you goodnight.'

She caught her breath. 'I want to kiss you goodnight too.'

'But you've set the rules. No kissing in private.'

She had to clear her throat to speak. 'I want

to say we don't need to enforce the rules yet, but I can't. I like kissing you, Josh. A lot. But I meant what I said the first night. We know where that kind of kissing will lead us and I don't want to go there.'

She couldn't deal with a no-strings fling with Josh. Not when he'd be going home soon. Not when she was starting to like him too much as a friend. To be honest, as more than a friend. Not when she realised if she didn't keep him at arm's length she could end up getting hurt.

'So we start as we mean to continue,' he said. 'No kissing in private.'

'That's right,' she said, unable to take her eyes from his sexy, sexy mouth, trembling inside from the need to press her mouth against his lips, to wind her arms around his neck and pull him close.

He dropped his hand. 'Then I'll just say goodnight.'

'Goodnight, Josh,' she said. 'I'll see you in the morning.'

She closed the door before she could change her mind. For a long moment she stood staring blindly at the door. Something told her that Josh was still on the other side and she had to fight the urge to call him back and tell him she'd changed her mind. She held her breath until she heard his footsteps moving slowly away and then let it out on a sigh of what she didn't know was relief or regret.

CHAPTER EIGHT

JOSH WAS THOROUGHLY enjoying his ride in Eloise's vintage sports car. For a car that was almost sixty years old it had a lot of power. Back home, he had driven a new model luxury European car ever since he could afford one. It was an outward flag of status to wave under the nose of the Boston family who had rejected him.

Yet this smart little white car garnered more attention from passers-by than any of his exceedingly expensive vehicles.

'A friend of my grandmother's put it up for sale when I'd barely got my driver's licence,' Eloise said. 'My grandmother knew how much I wanted it and lent me the money to get it. I paid her back every cent, of course.'

She'd been young to have been so sure of what she wanted. Yet he had known what he wanted when he'd been booted out of home at the age of sixteen: to show his former family they'd been wrong about him. He continued to pursue that aim with fierce determination.

'It's probably worth much more than you paid for it now,' he said.

'This car has been an excellent investment. New cars depreciate; this one continues to go up in value. Not that I'd ever sell it. I get stopped in the street by admirers all the time, with offers to buy it, offers to hire it.'

Jealousy, unexpected and shocking, hit him. Were the 'admirers' interested in the car or its beautiful driver? Even in the relatively subdued outfit she wore today, narrow-legged trousers in a mottled purple colour with a matching short jacket, she turned heads. Josh realised his fists were clenched tightly on his lap. He forced the feeling to go away. He had no claim on her whatsoever. 'Have you ever loaned the car out?'

'Just the once. To a movie production company. I knew someone there who begged me to borrow it and paid me a good fee. They returned it with a scratch on it and denied they'd put it there. My beloved car. Never again. I'm not known for my generosity in giving second chances.'

She said that last sentence in a lighthearted, almost throw-away manner. But he had no doubt she meant every word. Eloise was charming and fun, but you didn't get to run a successful business like hers with clients all around the world without a certain degree of toughness.

'I have, however, made a promise I intend to keep,' she continued. 'When Vinh decides to get married, I'll lend her my car for her wedding. Friendship trumps all.'

'Of course,' he said, thinking what a contradiction she was and how interesting it made her.

The wedding destination was on the outskirts of the town of Bowral in the southern highlands, south west of Sydney.

'I promise once we clear the city motorways the scenery will get interesting,' she said. 'Bowral is known as Double Bay in the country, as it's always been a rural retreat for wealthy Sydneysiders. The place is dotted with mansions on magnificent estates. Silver Trees, where the wedding is to be held, is one of them. It's been in the groom's family for ever…prize-winning gardens, an ornamental lake, expansive grounds, tennis court, swimming pavilion, stables, you name it—

all designed by a renowned architect in the nineteen-twenties.'

'I look forward to seeing it. I've never been outside of Sydney or Melbourne.'

'You didn't want to go up north to tropical Queensland for a holiday once you'd flown all the way here? An escape from the Boston winter perhaps?'

'I don't take holidays these days,' he said, more tersely than probably required.

'Fair enough,' she said. She drove in silence for a few minutes. 'Tell me, you asked me if I had childhood dreams of making wedding dresses for celebrities. I know your parents pretty much forced your hand to earn your own living. But was it your childhood ambition to be a billionaire tech mogul?'

He nearly choked from the shock of her blunt question. 'No one has ever asked me that before,' he said once he'd regained his voice.

She looked straight ahead as she spoke. 'Maybe because you seem quite formidable.'

'Formidable?'

'Your achievements are incredible. If I'd known who you were, I probably wouldn't have dared chat to you in the park.'

'I'm glad you did,' he said. Not for Tori's sake but for his own.

'Thanks to Daisy,' Eloise said lightly. 'But seriously, is that what you set out to be?'

'Does anyone actually set out to become that? I knew I wanted to work in the digital world, and planned on a degree in computer science, but that wasn't to be.'

'Because of what happened when you were sixteen?'

'It started even before then.' He paused. 'Do you really need to know all this?'

'If we were really engaged I'd already know it, wouldn't I?'

'I guess so,' he said grudgingly.

His past was his own private hell, not readily shared. But Eloise had a point: she would be expected to know more about him than she did if she was to be his future wife. *Wife*. He reeled at the thought, even in a hypothetical context.

He honestly didn't know why he had made that spontaneous offer of pretending to be her fiancé. It was all mixed up with his attraction to her, his loyalty to Tori, the fact that his time in Sydney was beginning to seem almost surreal. The meeting with the dog in the park. The paparazzi shot. The hilarity of being fitted for his tux in Eloise's studio. *These kinds of things did not happen to him.*

Then there had been the fantasy first meeting at Santa Monica they'd devised over a Thai take-out and a good Australian white wine. Against all logic, he'd found himself wishing that meeting had really happened. That he'd met Eloise somehow, somewhere, in a context that had nothing to do with Tori. And that he'd been a man open to love rather than one with a protective shield encasing his heart.

'Come on, spill,' she said. 'It can't be any more embarrassing than aspiring to be a mermaid.'

He couldn't help but smile at that. 'If you insist.'

'I do insist.'

'As I told you, even before I turned out to be genetically the wrong fit, I didn't fit the family mould. I showed no aptitude for the law or banking, the acceptable professions according to my ex-father.'

'You call him your *ex*-father?'

'What else fits? Technically my stepfather, I suppose, but that doesn't really apply, as he had no say in the matter. My mother tricked him into believing I was his own. I look at it as if he divorced me.'

I'm not your dad. You are nothing to do with me.

'I guess that's a valid way of putting it. By the way, he sounds utterly vile. How could you bring a boy up from a baby and then just turf him out? Weren't you his son in every way but by blood?'

'I don't think he particularly cared for me from the start, but he did his duty by me for sixteen years.'

'As he darn well should have, especially as he thought you were his own child,' she said indignantly.

He shrugged. 'Truth was, we never really clicked. I was a disappointment. Not academic. Certainly not a son to boast about at his club. When it came to career advice, he suggested I learn a trade, become an electrician or plumber. He'd say it with a sneer. Not that I thought there was anything wrong at all with learning a trade. I would have willingly done so. But he knew so little of who I was, he had no idea I was already supplementing my allowance by creating apps and trading gaming codes.'

'Your interests lay elsewhere.'

'In the burgeoning digital marketplace my conservative family barely acknowledged existed. Forget studying law at Harvard, I was destined to study at the Massachusetts Institute of Technology.' He paused. 'Until I wasn't. I was cut off with nothing, certainly no college fund.'

'The media calls you a self-made billionaire.'

'I don't deny the label. There was no one to give me a leg up. I got where I am under my own steam. I took risks, I had setbacks, but I pushed through. And I'm proud of it.'

'You've given your ex-father something to boast about now.'

He spoke through gritted teeth. 'I make very sure he knows what I've achieved. My ex-brother too. But neither of them would be boasting about me.'

A year ago, he'd seen his ex-father in the distance at the exclusive yacht club to which they both belonged. Josh was sure he'd seen him too but he'd turned away without acknowledging him. Not as his son, but not as his equal in the rich man's club. It had still hurt. And further fuelled his anger.

Eloise might think less of him if he admitted to the business deals he'd diverted from his brother, the wealthy clients he'd deflected from his father's law firm. She'd called him ruthless. She would be shocked if she knew just how ruthless. The power of having a lot of money had facilitated his actions. His fantasy wasn't of a happy-ever-after family reunion but of his father admitting he was wrong about him. As a teenager he'd been hurt and heartbroken at what his father and brother had done to him. As an adult, no love or respect remained, and he despised them for how they'd treated a kid who'd thought he belonged with them.

The car was stopped at traffic lights and Eloise turned to face him. Her expression was troubled. 'So when it boils down to it, your success has been fuelled by bitterness and revenge?'

'You could say that,' he said. 'Although it was sheer survival at first.'

'How good is that for you?'

'Satisfying in the extreme.'

'I mean for your health, your spiritual health if you like.' The lights changed and she faced the road again.

'I've never felt healthier,' he said, knowing that wasn't what she meant.

'For how long does it continue?' she said.

'I don't want to say the wrong thing here but surely your…your ex-father must see by now how wrong he was about you, how you might not have been born to his grand family but you were certainly worthy of it.'

The drive to prove himself had been his focus for so long, Josh didn't know how to think any other way. But when would enough be enough? 'I sometimes feel nothing I do would be enough to make him admit he was wrong.'

'He sounds a horrible man, not worthy of someone as brilliant as you. Why do you continue to seek his approval?'

'That's not what I'm doing,' he said tersely.

But underneath it all, was Eloise right? Was he still making a futile effort to seek the approval of that cold, unfeeling man who had kicked the boyish love he'd given so unstintingly as a child back in his teeth?

'That kind of negative emotion isn't good for a person. I know we don't know each other very well, but it makes me worry for you, Josh,' Eloise said. 'It cuts you off from the kinder side of life.'

A cold shiver ran up his spine at her words, the echo of Tori's. *I worry about you, Josh. You're cutting yourself off from life.*

'I can look after myself,' he said gruffly. 'I've been doing so for a long time.'

'I'm sure you can,' she said, with the resignation of someone who knew she was fighting a losing battle.

'Chalk that up to being another thing you now know about me,' he said.

'It's actually not something I'd be introducing into the conversation,' she said. 'That's your personal business.' An air of disapproval lingered for a long time in the car.

With the outskirts of Sydney left behind, the road took them through vast tracts of bushland, the green fields of dairy farms and horse studs, vineyards and turn-offs to historic villages with names like Berrima and Yerrinbool. 'The names are from the language of the people indigenous to this area,' Eloise explained.

'It's beautiful countryside,' he said.

'People drive out here for the day to visit antique shops, art galleries and wineries, inspect beautiful gardens, go horse riding or just to get out to the country. There are hotels and bed and breakfasts for longer stays. And there are some very popular wedding venues. It's lovely but I wouldn't want to live here. I'm a city girl myself.'

'I prefer the city too,' he said.

'Wait, I haven't asked where you live. I should know that.'

'My apartment is in the Seaport District, a penthouse with awesome views across the harbour. It's a relatively new area, redeveloped waterfront in South Boston. There are excellent restaurants and facilities and it's incredibly convenient for the business district and the airport, which makes it great for me.'

'What's your apartment like?'

'Very contemporary, all glass and stainless steel.' Lonely and empty might be the words he would also use to describe it. But he didn't want her to feel sorry for him. His life was exactly the way he wanted it to be. 'I don't know that you'd like it. It's nothing like your elegant apartment. I had an interior designer do it for me and I sometimes wonder if she took the "bachelor billionaire" brief too seriously.'

'I'm sure it's lovely.'

'It's actually quite sterile,' he said, surprising himself. 'I don't know why I live there actually, though it's already doubled in value. I keep gravitating back to the North End. You may remember it's a very old part of town.'

'I haven't been to Boston since my father

died, but I think I remember going there to a restaurant with my grandparents.'

'When my mother and I were evicted from the big house on Beacon Hill we went to live there with her sister, my Aunt Lily, in her apartment in Little Italy. The apartment was cramped and I had to go to a new high school, but I loved it.'

Eloise nodded thoughtfully. 'That's good information. If anyone asks I can maybe say we're thinking of moving to a house there instead of living in your bachelor apartment.'

'You'd like the area, I'm sure.'

All the best parts of his life were there. His Aunt Lily, who had given him a home. Tori's family trattoria and his close friendship with her family. Tori's bakery too; her spectacular cakes were to Boston's brides what Eloise's gowns were to Sydney's brides.

He could be himself there and judged for who he was and not by the size of his bank balance. So very different from the Boston where he had lived the first sixteen years of his life with his judgemental father whom nobody could please, not even his half-brother, who turned himself inside out in the process of trying. Warm, vibrant Eloise would fit right in in the North End. That she had ac-

tually been born in Boston would give her a
head start. But she was a Sydney person too,
with a thriving business she loved. A move
there couldn't possibly work.

Josh shook his head to clear it of the in-
vidious invasion of his thoughts. This fake
fiancé game was messing with his head. He
wasn't marrying Eloise, he wasn't dating
Eloise, and when she found out he'd been
hiding the truth about his visit to Sydney
and his knowledge of her long-lost twin he
wouldn't be talking to Eloise.

'Before we get there, I have a final question for you,' he said.

'Fire away,' she said.

'There's something I haven't asked you that
I should probably know. Why is a beautiful
woman like you without a date for this wedding? Without a real-life fiancé of her own
to accompany her? What went wrong with
your last guy?'

'He lied to me about who he really was,'
she said flatly. 'And that's unforgivable.'

'I see,' he said. He didn't need to know the
details. It just reinforced his earlier thoughts.

They were soon entering the salubrious
small town of Bowral, with shops and businesses lining the main road and those inter-

secting it. 'We've made good time,' Eloise said. 'Do you want to stretch your legs? Take a walk, grab a coffee in Bowral, even a bite of lunch, before we head to Silver Trees, which is on the other side of town?'

'Coffee sounds great,' he said. 'And now that you mention it, so does lunch.'

Eloise parked the car on the high street, so she could keep an eye on it, she said. Before she made to get out of the car she turned to him, her expression very serious. 'The fake engagement starts here. There are likely to be people I know in town for the wedding. Last chance for you to back out.'

'I'm in,' he said.

Even though she was the driver—no one, but *no one*, got to drive her precious vintage car—Josh insisted on getting out of the car first to come around to her side and open the door for her.

'I intend to start as I mean to continue as your fiancé,' he said.

She tensed. Thank heaven he hadn't said 'fake fiancé'. These streets could have ears. She would have to force herself to relax and trust him to play his part.

'Thank you,' she said.

It seemed the most natural thing in the world for him to take her hand as she walked with him towards her favourite Bowral café, which served great coffee and the most delicious pastries baked on the premises. Enfolding hers, his hand felt warm and large and somehow comforting. He was on her side, even for only a very limited time.

She was looking up at him and smiling at something he'd said when she heard her name called out. Eloise turned to see a woman she'd dressed for her wedding two years ago. All must be going well, as she was proudly sporting an advanced baby bump.

'Eloise, I thought it was you. Are you in town for Becca's wedding?' She didn't pause for an answer. 'Of course Becca would be wearing one of your gowns. For the second time, that is.'

'Anna, how lovely to see you.' They air kissed. 'And I can see congratulations are in order.'

The other woman smiled. 'Do you design christening gowns by any chance?'

'Only for my most special clients,' she said. 'Call me and we can chat.'

Eloise kept a special linen bag of offcuts from each wedding. They came in remarkably handy for creating baby outfits, both traditionally styled and contemporary, for christenings and naming ceremonies, made with the fabric from the mother's wedding dress. She didn't advertise the service, as there wasn't much profit in it, but it was an added extra for clients and unique, as far as she knew, to her company.

People boasted about starting their own christening gown family heirlooms. But you had to have bought a wedding gown from Eloise Evans Atelier first.

Anna was not doing a very good job of disguising her interest in the tall, handsome man standing by Eloise's side.

'Oh, Anna, this is my fiancé, Josh.'

The words tripped so easily off Eloise's tongue, thanks to a dint of practising in front of the mirror the previous night after Josh had gone home.

'Josh, this is Anna, one of my clients who had the most beautiful wedding two years ago.'

'Fiancé?' Anna said, sculpted eyebrows raised. 'But I heard...' She collected herself. 'Congratulations. How exciting.' Her gaze went straight to the ruby engagement ring glinting on Eloise's left hand. She seemed puzzled by it.

No doubt Anna had seen the horrible hashtags on *@lindytheblonde*'s social media. And believed every word. Yet here was wedding-hating Eloise Evans engaged to be married. You could almost see the cogs working in the woman's mind.

'It's only very recently that Ellie has done me the honour of agreeing to become my wife,' Josh said smoothly. He embellished his words by dropping a swift kiss on her cheek.

'Well, this is wonderful news,' said Anna.

'We certainly think so,' said Josh.

'Well played,' Eloise whispered, as Anna walked away. 'I dare say by the time we arrive at the wedding the word will have started to spread.'

'Piece of cake,' he said.

He reached for her hand again.

'And so it begins,' Eloise said, as if she were murmuring an endearment in her fiancé's ear.

CHAPTER NINE

As ELOISE SWUNG her little white sports car up the gravel driveway to her friend's soon-to-be husband's family estate, Silver Trees, Josh wondered what the hell he was doing there, ready to embark in full force on the fake fiancé scam. It went against the grain for him to out-and-out lie the way he had to that woman on the main street of Bowral.

And yet when Anna had given Eloise that look of sly surprise when told she was engaged, he'd felt a fierce surge of protectiveness. Obviously the woman was aware of the gossip being fomented by the heinous influencer who was trying to ruin Eloise out of meanness and spite. Perhaps Anna had even been guilty of spreading it. Eloise needed help. If that meant Josh acting the loving fiancé, then so be it. If she needed his help later to exact the kind of deeper revenge he'd outlined—and believed she should—he'd be on call to guide her.

One thing was for sure—Eloise had better restrain him if he found himself anywhere near that *@lindytheblonde*, as heaven knew what words he might unleash on her.

Eloise did not deserve such meanness. They'd had a rapid getting-to-know-you process over the last few days. He had noted how thoughtful and caring she was towards others. That had led him to wonder who cared for her? It seemed she went home to that stylish apartment by herself every night to lavish love on Daisy, the little stray dog who had been instrumental in his meeting Eloise. But who lavished love on Eloise? He couldn't offer love, but he could offer his help in stopping this unfair attack on her livelihood. He vowed to do his utmost to be an impeccable fake fiancé.

Eloise pulled over in the designated parking area for the select group of guests who had been invited to stay at the house. She turned off the engine, put the stick shift into gear, and pulled on the quaint, old-fashioned handbrake. It was one cool car. She turned to Josh.

'About the accommodation,' she said. He

got the impression she had been building up to saying this and now had to let it out.

'Yes?' he said.

'When I told Becca I would, after all, be bringing a plus-one, and my plus-one was actually my fiancé, she was delighted for me and assumed you'd be staying in my room. The thing is, the room I've stayed in here a few times before is very small.'

Josh had wondered at the sleeping arrangements but hadn't felt he could ask for details. She'd just mentioned they would be staying at the house where the wedding would be taking place. 'I could always book into a hotel in town. I'm sure it's not too late to get a room somewhere.'

She frowned. 'That wouldn't send the right message, would it? Not for a newly engaged couple supposedly madly in love.'

'No, it wouldn't. And we need to appear genuine.'

'I'm glad you think so too. But sharing this room might not be so bad. It must have been originally a child's room, I think. There's a single bed and a sofa. I'm happy to sleep on the sofa and give you the bed. Even then it might be a bit of a squash for a man but it's comfortable enough and—'

Josh put up his hand. 'I insist on taking the sofa. No further argument.'

It was a relief, in a way, that there was only a single bed. He wouldn't be taunted by the fact he couldn't share the bed with her.

'You're the one doing me a favour. I insist on you having the bed.'

The interior of the car was thick with unspoken words and denials and a simmering undercurrent of sexual tension centring around the word *bed*. The mere thought of the enforced intimacy of sharing a bedroom with her was arousing. Eloise in her nightwear, Eloise naked under the shower, Eloise there with him all night long. But he could not think like that.

To keep his equilibrium, he had to act as if they were platonic friends bunking down together to save costs in a backpackers' hostel. He'd certainly done that back before he started to make serious money. But not with a woman he found so intensely desirable. Not with a woman who was forbidden to him in so many ways. He felt sure she felt the same undeniable physical attraction, and had her own reasons for fighting it.

'A gentleman would take the sofa,' he said through gritted teeth.

He hadn't meant to use the word *gentle-man* in that context, as he had in the fiction they had devised to explain their first meeting. And their play on his gentlemanly—or, rather more importantly, his ungentlemanly behaviour. There'd been a distinct flirtatious undercurrent to that conversation—on both sides. But that was only talk. This situation was real and forced them into an uncomfortably intimate proximity.

'If we can't agree, why don't we toss a coin for who gets the bed when we get to the room?' she said.

'We'll see about that,' he said. No way would he allow her to sleep on a sofa. He could sleep on the floor if he had to.

'I didn't realise how stubborn you could be,' she said, obviously bemused.

He grinned. 'You've got that right. Although I'd say determined rather than stubborn.'

As it turned out, she needn't have worried about who was or wasn't going to get the bed versus the sofa. The Silver Trees housekeeper led them into the lift and onto the first floor. The woman opened the door to a luxurious room with an enormous king-size bed and an en-suite bathroom. French doors opened out to a balcony and a view of the garden.

Eloise stared at the housekeeper in ill-disguised dismay. 'But this isn't my usual room.'

Josh followed her gaze to the enormous bed that dominated the room. There was no sofa, just a big vintage cane chair that looked exceedingly uncomfortable. But they couldn't display misgivings. As far as their hosts were concerned, he and his fiancée should be delighted to have that big bed.

He put his arm around Eloise and squeezed her shoulder, hoping she'd get the message she was giving the game away by her show of reluctance.

'I was told to swap you to this larger guest room, as your fiancé was with you,' the housekeeper said, obviously confused by the lack of enthusiasm.

'It's a marvellous room, isn't it, honey?' Josh said.

Eloise's eyes widened at his use of the endearment. But he was taking the role of fake fiancé and running with it.

She caught on. 'Yes. It's a beautiful room,' she gushed.

'And so good of you to organise it for us at such short notice,' Josh said.

The housekeeper looked gratified.

When he was growing up their house-keeper had been a very nice woman. She'd even cried when he and his mother had left. But she'd been too scared of losing her job to come and see them at his new home.

'We're thrilled,' Eloise said, right into the act now. 'Thank you. And thank you to Mr and Mrs Sanderson for giving us such a beautiful room. We'll be very comfortable here.'

Comfortable? He had to fight the images of him and Eloise making very good use of that bed. There wouldn't be a lot of sleeping going on, that was for sure. He wanted her. Badly. But the reasons for it not being a good idea for him to make love with her were still there, clamouring at him to keep his gaze away from the bed and the tantalising possibilities it evoked.

'Do you need help with your luggage?' asked the housekeeper.

'No, thank you, we can get it ourselves,' said Eloise very quickly.

Josh watched with Eloise until the house-keeper disappeared into the lift and they saw no one else was in earshot.

She turned to him. 'Only one bed. Not even a sofa. What the heck are we going to do?'

'I'll sleep on the chair. Or the floor.'

'No, you won't. I can't let you do that. Either way would be hideously uncomfortable and totally unfair to you when you're doing me a favour. The bed is huge; we'll just have to both sleep in it, trying…trying not to be aware the other person is there.'

'Are you serious? Do you honestly think I could sleep in a bed with you and not be aware you were there?' An image of her flashed into his mind, of her lying back against the rumpled sheets, her dark hair spilled across the pillows, her shoulders bare, her breasts… Her warm, sexy presence would be the only thing on his mind. 'That won't be easy.'

She looked up at him, her blue eyes huge, her cheeks flushed. 'It won't be easy for me either, Josh. Please be aware of that.'

Did she realise that knowing she wanted him as much as he wanted her did nothing to make it easier for him? She looked so woebegone he couldn't stop himself from opening his arms. 'Come here,' he said. She went towards him and he enfolded her in a comforting hug. It wasn't breaking her rule. They weren't behind closed doors. To anyone seeing them, they were an engaged couple embracing.

'This is going to be more difficult than I

thought,' she said, her voice muffled against his shoulder. 'Look how I missed that cue from you back then. The housekeeper must have thought I was very odd not to exclaim in delight at the beautiful room in this amazing mansion. I told you I wasn't a good actor.'

He pulled back from the hug so that, while she still stood within the circle of his arms, he could look down into her lovely face. 'You're doing fine,' he said. 'It will be worth it. Just think of the damage that influencer woman is doing to your business.'

'More cancellations this morning. Vinh texted me before I picked you up.'

'Put them right back on the bottom of your waiting list when they call wanting to be reinstated, which they will do once they realise they've been suckered.'

'I wouldn't do that.'

His voice hardened. 'I would. I told you, I'm vengeful. Loyalty should be rewarded. Not betrayal. How stupid of them to be influenced by that—'

'That *influencer.*'

'That's the word.'

She laughed and he felt her relax.

'Let's try and have fun with this,' he said. 'From what you say, it's going to be a great party. Let's enjoy it, at the same time knowing we're sticking it to an enemy of your business. Nothing can be more satisfying than that.'

Despite Eloise's protests, Josh insisted on carrying her overnight bag as well as his own while she carried her long dress in a special Eloise Evans Atelier garment bag to their room. He didn't have to pretend to be a gentleman, she thought, it was obviously innate to him. But she couldn't help her thoughts from straying to what he would be like when he was being ungentlemanly. In this very room.

She did her best to ignore the contentious bed while she hung her dress alongside Josh's tuxedo in a matching bag in the wardrobe. She walked over to stand beside him where he stood looking out of the French doors. They opened out to a wide balcony edged with lavishly planted containers and across the garden to the green fields studded with grazing horses.

'It's an awesome view,' he said.

'The other side of the house, where the family have their rooms, overlooks the lake and the stand of silver birch trees that gives the house its name. This house is incredible, yet it's a family home. I grew up in a comfortable house in Sydney's inner west, near Sydney University, where my father taught. I can't imagine what it must have been like for Simon to grow up with something like this.' She faltered to a halt. 'I'm sorry, Josh, you must have lived in a wonderful house before you had to move.'

'Home was a grand townhouse with a view to Boston Common. My grandparents—ex-grandparents—had a place something like this in Northborough, about an hour out of Boston, that we used to visit. But there are few happy memories. And now I can buy any house I choose to.'

'Which is a triumph in itself,' she said, not certain what else to say.

'I guess it is,' he said.

Not for the first time, Eloise thanked her lucky stars for the stability of the childhood her happily married parents had given her. She'd long stopped wondering what her life with her birth mother might have been like. However, she sometimes wondered if her parents' romance had given her unrealistic expectations of relationships. She'd had her heart crushed a few times by seeing in a man what she wanted him to be, not who he actually was. Craig had played her by pretending to be someone he wasn't. He'd outright lied and, at the beginning, she'd been so besotted she hadn't seen the signs. No wonder she was wary of taking a man at face value.

'Will you be okay here by yourself?' she asked Josh. 'I have to go and check everything is perfect with Becca's dress and the bridesmaids' dresses. There are only two bridesmaids and a flower girl. Believe it or not, this is a relatively low-key wedding compared to some, as it's her second. But it's Simon's first and he wanted a big celebration. As you said, it looks to be quite a party.'

'I'm perfectly fine by myself. I'll see you when you get back.'

'I won't be long,' she said.

There was an awkward moment when she wanted to lean up and kiss him on the cheek but decided against it. *No kissing in private.*

CHAPTER TEN

FROM THE MOMENT Josh had first laid eyes on Eloise in the park with Daisy he had thought her to be an exceptionally beautiful woman. But nothing had prepared him for the sight of Eloise dressed for the wedding.

Already in his new tux, he'd gone out on the balcony and turned his back while she got ready. It had seemed way too intimate to be in the same room as her while she got dressed. Not that she used the bedroom for changing—the bathroom was there for that. No, it was the private female rituals that only a woman's lover would usually witness that he found too disconcerting, the primping and preening and perfecting.

What had made him decide to leave the room was when she, dressed modestly in a satin robe patterned with oriental dragons, had leaned in close to the mirror to fasten her outsize earrings. The hairdresser and make-up artist employed by the bride had done her hair and make-up, and Eloise's thick dark hair had been swept up into a glamorous style. As she'd peered into the mirror her robe had slipped off her shoulders to reveal the nape of her neck, slender and pale. She'd seemed somehow vulnerable and exposed, yet deeply sensual at the same time. He'd been swept by the desire not just to protect her but also to make her his, and he'd had to fight the impulse to press a tender kiss to the base of her delicate nape and slide the robe all the way down off her shoulders.

Instead he'd muttered an excuse that he needed to get some fresh air and headed out onto the balcony. It had been left to his imagination to guess what else she was doing in there—was she wearing anything under that robe?—and his imagination tantalised him. But not once had he looked back to catch a glimpse of her getting dressed. He respected her privacy and dignity too much for that.

Then she was at the French windows. 'I'm ready when you are,' she said.

He turned. And could do nothing but stare. His heart started to thud into overdrive and his mouth went dry. She stood in a strapless dress that cupped her breasts, then hugged the curves of her body to her hips before it floated down in a series of layers—he wasn't sure what you'd call them…flounces maybe?—to the floor. The dress was an iridescent deep blue that picked up the light and shimmered through subtle tones of purple and violet. The colour contrasted with the creaminess of her skin and complemented the cornflower blue of her eyes.

Her black hair was twisted and turned up on her head and, with her deep red lips and highlighted eyes, she looked like some Hollywood movie star of a time long before she was born. Glittering clear stones hung from her ears but she wore no other jewellery save the ruby ring that shone brighter in contrast to the blue dress. He had never seen a more beautiful woman.

He stared at her for so long, she shifted from high-heeled shoe to high-heeled shoe. 'Do I look all right?' How could she imagine for even a second that she would ever look anything but much more than 'all right'?

'You look absolutely beautiful,' he said hoarsely. 'You just need long gloves and a jewelled cigarette holder to look like you stepped out of a vintage movie.'

She smiled, pleased. 'But if I wore the long gloves it would cover my ring, and what would be the point of that? And of course I don't smoke.'

'You look…breathtaking. Are you sure you won't outshine the bride?'

Eloise laughed. 'No one could outshine the bride! Her gown is exquisite and she's glowing with happiness.'

She picked up a filmy blue wrap and a small beaded purse from the bed. 'We don't want to be late.'

'It's an honour to escort you, Eloise. Truly.'

'I'm glad you're here. I wouldn't have worn such a glamorous dress if I'd come on my own,' she said. 'And may I say how handsome you look in your tux?'

'That's really thanks to you and your team,' he said.

'I don't know about that,' she said. 'I think the very good-looking man wearing the tux is what makes it look so good. They say clothes maketh the man, but in your case I'd say the man maketh the tux.'

He laughed. 'If you say so.' He liked her quirky outlook. Honestly, he'd never met a woman like her. Tori was her lookalike, of course, but they were so very different in personality. Eloise was incomparable.

Josh offered her his arm. 'Let's go and give that troublemaker influencer something to think about.'

'Like how to backpedal out of the lies she's spread about me.'

She tucked her hand into his arm and looked up at him. Again he caught his breath at how lovely she looked, how alluring with the subtle curves of her breasts, the shadow of her cleavage revealed by the strapless gown. 'It would be a different scenario all together if you weren't with me, Josh. Thank you again for being here.'

He couldn't think of anywhere else he would rather be.

Eloise had never felt more confident entering a room of people than with Josh by her side. Together they walked into the ballroom of the mansion, which had been set up for the marriage service with rows of white chairs forming an aisle and facing the front of the room. While the overwhelming focus of the wedding guests' interest was on the bride, Eloise soon became aware that her appearance with Josh was causing a secondary

ripple of interest. She knew they were noticed as a couple and comments made, and
she'd detected several glances towards her
left hand. By the time she and Josh made
their way to their seats for the ceremony,
she felt satisfied the news of her 'engagement' was spreading.

Because she knew several of the bride's
friends, and had dressed others as either
brides or bridesmaids, Eloise knew quite a
number of the other guests. She didn't look
out for @lindytheblonde but she knew she
must be there.

If she didn't have to see the woman ever
again she would be grateful. She just wanted
her nemesis to know that the basis of her attack had now been proved to be erroneous.
Eloise was here with an incredibly handsome
'fiancé' and looking her best in a killer dress
from her own label. The bride and her attendants were dressed in the most exquisite,
money-no-object dresses from Eloise Evans
Atelier. That should be enough. If not…well,
Josh had presented her with a next-step option she would shudder to take.

She settled in to enjoy the wedding, Josh by
her side. No matter her opinion about a wedding for herself, there was something about

other people's weddings that always grabbed at her emotions. The favourite part of any ceremony for Eloise was to see the bride come down the aisle and then watch for the moment when her groom first caught sight of her. In this case Simon didn't disappoint with a look of wonder and love when he saw Becca walking up the aisle towards him, the joy shining from her.

It brought the sting of tears to Eloise's eyes. But beyond her usual sentimentality and happiness for her friends, she felt a deep and heartfelt yearning of her own. *Would it ever be her?* Not so much the dress and the flowers and all the fuss, but would a man ever look at her like that? And would she ever be able to trust a man enough to look at him with such unreserved love? For a deeply disconcerting moment she imagined that man was Josh and had to shake the image from her mind.

She clasped his hand tightly. 'I told you I always cry at weddings,' she whispered.

Eloise sniffled her way through the rest of the ceremony. Becca's first marriage had been short and miserable and her friend had vowed never to let a man into her life again. Then she'd met Simon, and risked her heart a second time. How had she found the strength to do that?

The ceremony over, the bride and groom walked triumphantly back down the aisle as husband and wife. Eloise realised she had been holding on tight to Josh's hand the entire time. He pulled a handkerchief—a crisp, white, old-fashioned handkerchief—from his pocket.

'You might need this,' he said quietly.

Her hands flew to her face. 'Panda eyes?'

He nodded. She scrubbed under her eyes with the handkerchief where she thought the smeared mascara must be.

'Let me,' he said, taking it back. She tilted her face upwards. Gently he wiped beneath one eye then another. She sat perfectly still, hardly daring to breathe. Loving his touch, even masked by a handkerchief. He sat back to look critically at his work. 'Better,' he said. 'Although you look beautiful even with panda eyes.'

'Thank you,' she said.

She smiled, he smiled too, and their eyes met for a long moment. Was he acting? Without thinking, she leaned across and kissed him on the mouth, a sweet, tender kiss of thanks, of gratitude, of sheer appreciation of how thoughtful he was. It wasn't staged. She meant it and she was smiling as she pulled away. He was smiling too and there was something warm and questioning she hadn't seen before in his eyes that sent a tremor of awareness through her. Josh took her hand again and she squeezed it tightly as they rose from their seats. The truth hit her with painful clarity—the truth she had been refusing to acknowledge.

She could so easily fall in love with this man.

But Eloise did not want to fall in love with a man she scarcely knew. She had to slam down hard on that inner voice that cajoled, *You've known him long enough.* She'd listened to that voice before with disastrous consequences. Right now, however, she wasn't going to fight it, just ignore it. Josh had suggested they relax, have fun and enjoy the party, and that was exactly what she intended to do.

The guests flocked around the bride and groom. Eloise and Josh waited their turn. Congratulations were said. Introductions were made. And Josh played the doting fiancé to perfection. 'You deserve someone like Josh,' murmured Becca. 'Well done for opening your heart again to love.'

Only of course she hadn't and her heart was still shut down to love. Everything about her and Josh being together was a sham. She was pretending to be in love to save her bridal business. How hypocritical of her was that? And he… She wasn't really sure why he had offered to help her. Could it be simply because he enjoyed exacting revenge for revenge's sake? Even when it was someone else's revenge? In spite of the ruthlessness he'd demonstrated, she couldn't bring herself to believe that of Josh. Not the Josh who was so sweet to Daisy and had been so kind to her. She had to tell herself it was because of a gentlemanly instinct. And she was just so glad he was here with her.

The bride and groom disappeared for more photos. The guests were directed into the large conservatory where first cocktails and then a sit-down dinner were to be served. Eloise was greeted by some women she knew quite well, and some she didn't know so well. Congratulations on her engagement flowed and Josh was given appraising and approving looks. She was gratified by people's happiness for her and dreaded how uncomfortable it would be to say, a few months down the track, that her long-distance engagement had, as it happened, not worked out.

But right now, she and Josh had their answers ready.

'Yes, a November wedding, we think,' she said.

'Boston is home for me, but then, it used to be home for Ellie too, so we're keeping our options open.'

'I have no intention of closing my business— never, ever. Oh, you're on my waiting list? Don't worry, I won't be too distracted by my own wedding to design you a fabulous wedding gown.'

'Yes, I knew she was "the one" straight away. How? I…uh…just knew.'

'You know I dressed Roxee and her wedding party? Josh and I first met when I was in Los Angeles for the wedding.'

'Yes, we have kept it quiet,' Josh said. 'We wanted to be sure.'

'Thank you. You're very kind to say we look like we're made for each other.'

'No, I don't have a brother just like me back home in Boston.'

'Oh, yes, Josh is a keeper.'

'Ellie is a keeper for sure.'

She found it emotionally draining to keep

up the act and not slip and was glad when they were asked to head to their assigned tables for the speeches and dinner.

They were nearly at their table, when Eloise clutched Josh's arm. 'Don't look now but she's over there…*@lindytheblonde*.'

'Is she watching us?'

'If looks could kill…'

Josh pulled her close to him and looked deeply into her eyes, smoothing a wisp of hair that had tugged free from her updo as only a lover would do. 'Do I look suitably smitten?' he said in a voice only she could hear.

'I thought you said you were a terrible actor?' she murmured. 'Because you're being very convincing.'

He came closer, so close she felt giddy from his scent, weak at the knees from the contact. 'Maybe it's because I'm not acting,' he said, in a voice so low she wasn't sure she heard him correctly.

She didn't have a chance to ask him to repeat it because suddenly the influencer was at her elbow. 'I hear congratulations are in order,' she said with an insincere smile from her trout mouth's inflated lips that didn't reach her eyes.

'Yes,' Eloise said simply. She introduced

her to Josh and the woman's eyes narrowed at the same time she mouthed platitudes. Josh acted the proud, loving fiancé as if he'd been born to it.

When Eloise had first read the influencer's mean social media posts, calculated to ruin her business, she had lain awake planning exactly what she'd say to this woman if she got the chance. Now she kept her mouth shut. Josh had, instead, offered her a way to defuse her accusations. Then *@lindytheblonde* introduced her and Josh to her fiancé.

Immediately, Eloise recognised his name. One of her clients had cancelled her wedding when she'd discovered both his cheating and his over-active interest in her wealthy father's bank balance. A schoolfriend had also dated him and could only say he was bad news. Perhaps it was karma, perhaps the influencer and her fiancé had met their match. But Eloise decided she'd be the better person and graciously accepted her congratulations while giving congratulations of her own.

'What was that about?' Josh said in an undertone when the influencer had gone. 'I was looking forward to watching you stick the knife into that awful, supercilious woman and twist it.'

'Because, darling Josh, sometimes karma takes hold of the knife and twists it for you. I'd rather have one night of being your pretend fiancée than a lifetime of being a wife to that guy. I almost feel sorry for her. Almost.'

'You'll have to explain that one to me later,' he said. 'It doesn't sound enough like revenge to me.' He looked so puzzled she had to kiss him again.

'Thank you, thank you…' she murmured against his mouth.

All the while she couldn't stop wondering if she had correctly heard Josh. Had he really said he wasn't acting? And if so, what could he have meant by it?

CHAPTER ELEVEN

JOSH USUALLY WENT out of his way to avoid weddings. A generous cheque and an apology for his inability to attend was his stock response to an invitation. But to his surprise he found himself enjoying this wedding. The other guests on the table were pleasant company. The meal was superb. The speeches, usually interminable, were short, warm and witty. Just the kind of speeches he would like to have at his own wedding. He pulled up his thoughts. When had he started thinking there might actually be a wedding for him one day in the distant future, instead of never?

The answer was sitting next to him. *Eloise*. Enchanting, funny, gorgeous Eloise. He was getting in deeper every minute he spent in her company. Maybe he'd imbibed one too many toasts to the bride and groom with the plentiful French vintage champagne. Or the excellent Australian red wine with dinner before that. But the more he pretended to be in love with Eloise, the more he started to wonder what was stopping him from considering the actual possibility. Not of a real-life engagement. Of course not. But of somehow seeing more of her. Long-distance dating, even. Because he was thoroughly enjoying every minute of her company. And he dreaded having to say goodbye. A life without Eloise in it seemed somehow unacceptable.

She excused herself to go to the powder room in the company of one of the other women at the table. Immediately after she left her chair, he felt bereft. He watched that delightful sway of her hips as she walked away, the way she leaned down to smile at something her companion was saying. He could not keep his eyes off her.

Hurry back to me, Ellie.

Again he had that surreal feeling that, since he'd been in Australia, the foundations of his life were shifting on ground that had suddenly become unstable. His rules against a serious relationship were self-imposed. But then, he'd always been perfectly satisfied without a committed, meaningful connection with a woman.

Eloise had commented that his life was motivated by bitterness and revenge. He had proudly owned the truth of it. But spending time with Eloise was making him question that truth. Had the time passed for focusing his entire life on the relentless pursuit of extreme wealth to prove he was worthy of the old life of his childhood? Was he letting the cruelty of his father cut him off from what Eloise called 'the kinder side of life'?

His rules had been forged when he was sixteen, bewildered and hurting from the out-of-the-blue total rejection of his father. Now, four months away from the age of thirty, a new thought was percolating through: the best revenge against that cold-hearted man might be a life well lived. Personal fulfilment could be a fine shield against cruelty and rejection. What was stopping him?

Only his own old fears.

Perhaps it was time to flick the switch, to think forward to how he might treat his own son or daughter one day rather than back on how his father had treated him. *Kids?* He was thinking *kids?* He shook his head. That took reconsidering his life too far. There'd been some funny, teasing speeches about babies directed at the newlyweds. That must be where the thought had come from. He shoved it right back.

Eloise slid back into her chair beside him just as the band struck up. She held on to his shoulder as she settled into her chair. He reached up to hold her hand and she squeezed it. She was just playing her part as fake fiancée. He knew that. Yet with it came a thrill of possession as she left her hand in his.

The bride and groom danced their first dance together as husband and wife. Gradually the ballroom—cleared now of chairs— filled up with couples dancing. Josh turned to Eloise and saw that she was swaying in time to the music. He asked her to dance and they joined the other couples on the floor.

'You can waltz,' she said.

'So can you.'

'My grandmother said it was a desirable skill for a young lady. She taught me. It felt very strange when I first waltzed with a boy instead of an old lady.'

He laughed. How often had he laughed since he'd met her? More than in the previous six months, he felt sure. Laughter was meant to release feel-good endorphins. Maybe that was what was making him start to re-evaluate his life strategy. It couldn't be that other word starting with *L*. 'Your grandmother sounds like an interesting woman.'

'She was; we were very close—she and my mother too.' Eloise's glance went to the ruby ring. 'Where did you learn to dance?'

'At my old private school. Very unwillingly, I might add.'

She laughed and he whirled her around the dance floor. Perhaps because of his avoidance of weddings, where old-fashioned dancing still seemed to hold sway, he had forgotten how intimate a waltz could be. As intimate and exciting as an embrace.

He was intensely aware of where his body connected with Eloise's, of her warmth and curves. His arm around her waist held her close, her hand rested on his shoulder, her cheek felt smooth and cool against his cheek. Her scent was already familiar, rich and sweet and intoxicating. Other couples danced around them but he was scarcely aware of their presence—he was too lost in the rhythm of his private dance with Eloise.

It was part of wedding protocol that the bride and groom made their way around the dance floor to dance in turn with each of their guests. Josh smiled when they broke in on his dance with Eloise but in truth he felt like growling. He didn't want to let her go.

Eloise waltzed away with Simon, and Josh took his turn to dance with Becca. He held her at a polite distance. Even for a duty dance he did not want another woman in his arms, even a bride so obviously crazy about her new husband. 'A great wedding,' he said. 'The best I've ever been to, in fact.'

'Thank you,' Becca said. 'We're so glad you were able to come with lovely Eloise. What a gem of a woman she is, in every way.'

'Yes,' he said. 'She is that.'

Becca laughed. 'You don't have to try to chat.'

'What do you mean?'

'You haven't taken your eyes off her since you relinquished her to Simon. You've got it bad, haven't you?'

It? He remembered his role as fake fiancé. 'Yes, I have. I…uh…had a crush on her the moment I met her.' And just maybe that wasn't a fib. But a crush was just a crush.

Becca smiled. 'You can't hide how you feel about her. I can see it in your eyes. Love is hard to find and to be cherished. Simon and

I wish you both the kind of happiness we've found.'

Josh was too stupefied to find an answer for her. Thankfully he didn't have to, as Simon waltzed Eloise back to him. 'I'm returning your beautiful fiancée into your care,' he said.

Josh gladly took her back into his arms but he was too shaken by what Becca had said to think straight. He just held Eloise close and kept on waltzing.

Dancing with Josh was utter bliss. From the waltz, to the classic rock, to the crazy group dances that only half the guests knew the steps of, Josh had rhythm. He had rhythm, he had energy, he had the moves. And they moved well together. Not only was he hot, but also he was fun. There were times Eloise forgot their engagement was fake, and that the relationship was staged, his mock affection seemed so real. And that was dangerous. Although she suspected he felt the same physical attraction she felt for him. That was more difficult to fake.

Early on in the evening, she'd gone past being on edge, worrying he or she might trip up on an answer about their engagement or wedding plans. However, people asked basically the same questions and the answers almost came by rote. They didn't trip up once.

She'd only sipped at a flute of champagne for the toasts—just in case there was another encounter with the influencer she wanted to keep a clear head. But *@lindytheblonde* had steered clear of her. So she couldn't blame champagne for the recklessness of her rising desire for Josh. She knew their time together was limited and she wanted him. Perhaps she wanted him so badly *because* their time was limited.

The band were playing the final set of slow dances. The bride had changed into her going-away dress—designed by Eloise Evans Atelier, of course—and she and her new husband were saying their final farewells to a group of their elderly relatives. Soon the wedding would be over.

'We haven't talked about what happens after tonight,' Eloise said in a low murmur.

'Again we stick to something close to the truth. It's a long-distance engagement. We just keep quiet about it until—'

'Until it becomes too hard, as long-distance relationships tend to do.'

'It quietly fizzles out.'

'Although we tried so hard to make it work.'

'All that,' he said.

They both dwindled away to silence. 'This is too gloomy for words,' she said. 'Can we forget about tomorrow when we've still got today to enjoy?'

And tonight ahead of us, she thought, thinking of that big bed with a shiver of anticipation. How would she be able to resist the temptation of having him so close?

She laid her head on his shoulder and they swayed together to the medley of classic love songs, thigh to thigh, hip to hip as she dreamed silly daydreams about what might be if things were different with Josh. Then the music stopped and they gathered with the other guests to farewell the bride and groom. There was an awkward moment when Becca and Simon had gone and people started to leave as the band announced the final number. Lights were lowered for the last dance.

'Do you know how many women here have asked if my dress is for sale?' she said. 'Not this exact one, of course, but one of the same design. Or they've asked if I make it in white as a wedding dress. I haven't been actively looking for business, but it's come my way. I'm thinking maybe I should branch out with a party dress diffusion line or maybe...' There was something intent in his eyes that made her falter to a halt.

'It's a superb dress,' he said. He lowered his head to hers so only she could hear. 'It looks sexy as hell on you. But I can't stop wondering how it would look off you.'

'Oh,' she said, a tingle of want tightening her nipples and running down her spine.

'I've offended you,' he said. 'Taken the game too far.'

'No. Not at all,' she said breathlessly. 'You didn't offend me.'

'But I've overstepped the mark. I'll sleep out on the balcony with the plants tonight.'

'It'll be too cold. It's several degrees colder here than it is in Sydney.'

'Then I'll sleep in the car.'

'You won't fit,' she said. She wound her arms around his neck and pressed close to him as they swayed to the slow, romantic music in the darkened room. 'I'm afraid it will have to be the bed for you tonight.' She pressed her lips to his. Then she couldn't wait for the band to finish and for the lights to come on, to have to make farewells to the people she knew.

With a low murmur of invitation, she took his hand and led him from the ballroom.

CHAPTER TWELVE

ELOISE THREW HER inhibitions away as soon as the ballroom was behind her. Forget her 'no kissing in private' rule. Whatever had made her impose that dictate? Kissing Josh was a delicious pastime to be enjoyed whenever she found the opportunity. She wanted Josh and she could see no real reason why she shouldn't have him. If only just for the night.

They kissed and laughed and stumbled as they tried to walk at the same time as kiss, all the way back to their room, only stopping when there was another couple waiting for the small lift. Josh made a grand gesture to usher them—Becca's cousin and his girlfriend—into the lift ahead of them. Who cared if her lipstick was smeared from passionate kissing and she was hanging on to Josh as if she never wanted to let him go? To all intents and purposes *they were engaged* and acting entirely appropriately.

Once they reached their room, Josh slammed the door shut behind them. He pushed her against the wall and held her hands above her head with one of his big hands as he kissed her—hard, hungry, urgent. She kissed him back with equal urgency, meeting his tongue with hers, straining her body against his. He ran his other hand down her bare arms, the sides of her breasts, and she trembled at the pleasure of it. She wanted him so much it was a physical ache.

He kissed down the side of her neck to the hollow of her throat and she murmured her pleasure. Her breasts swelled above the top of the bodice of her dress. She ached for him to touch her. Forget caution, forget worry about how this might end, her world shrank to just him and her and how he made her feel, her need for more. *Josh.*

She attempted to hook one leg around his in an effort to get closer but her dress, tightly fitted to her hips, got in the way.

He released her arms. 'This dress needs to come off,' he said, his voice husky.

'Yes,' she said.

'Do you want that?'

'Yes, yes and yes again,' she said impatiently.

Desire had been relentlessly building since that first dance. The way he moved, the way he held her so close, so possessively. It might not be anything more than this night but she would regret it if she didn't take full advantage of his willingness, of that big, inviting bed.

'You're sure?'

'I told you what kissing like that would lead to. And I want— Oh!'

He deftly turned her around and kissed the nape of her neck, the backs of her ears. How did he know that was one of her secret turn-on spots?

Then he slowly pulled down the back zip of her dress. The dress was lined with fine silk and it was like an extra caress on her highly sensitised skin as it fell from her body to pool on the floor.

She stepped out of her gown and moved it aside so she stood in just her deep blue lace thong, a strapless bra and her glittering high-heeled stilettos. From behind, Josh caressed her back and started to unhook her bra, but she twisted in his arms to face him.

'My turn now,' she said, her breath coming unevenly, scarcely able to get the words out.

She planted small kisses over his face as, with impatient fingers that weren't quite steady, she undid the buttons of his jacket and slid it off his shoulders.

'It was fun to fit you for this jacket, but it's even more fun to take it off you,' she murmured as she placed it on the chair near the bed. Even giddy with desire and want, she couldn't throw that beautiful piece of tailoring on the floor. With impatient fingers she unfastened the studs and buttons of his dress shirt and slid it off his broad shoulders as he freed his arms from the sleeves.

She stilled as she took in the delicious sight of him, wearing only his trousers, broad-shouldered, well-built, skin smooth and lightly tanned.

'Do I pass inspection?' he said.

'Oh, yes,' she sighed, placing her hands flat on his muscular chest to slide them down his flat, washboard stomach. 'Are you really and truly a tech nerd? Because you look more like an athlete to me.'

'Both,' he said shortly, his breath coming faster as her hands went lower.

'And here I was thinking you couldn't get any better looking.' Her voice broke. 'You're perfect.'

'I don't know about that,' he said, scarcely able to get the words out as she slipped her fingers under the waistline of his trousers, then went to undo his belt. 'Are you teasing me? Keep doing that and I—'

'Won't be responsible for what happens next?' Eloise looked up flirtatiously at him, not hiding the need from her voice. 'I'm looking forward to that.' She started to unbuckle his belt.

'Two can play at this game,' he said hoarsely as he unhooked her bra and tossed it onto the bed. He gazed at her in wonder, standing there in just her thong and her glittering stilettos. 'You're the one with the perfect body. *Ellie,*' he groaned.

She didn't let many people call her *Ellie* but she had given him permission and she liked how her name sounded when he said it in his deep voice.

He stroked her breasts, rolling her nipples between his fingers until they were hard and aching. As he slid his hands down her waist, her muscles contracted with pleasure and anticipation. He slipped his fingers under the scrap of lace that was her thong and she gasped. He would find her ready for him. What else had that slow, sensuous dancing been but a subtle and exquisite form of foreplay?

She unfastened his trousers and started to push them down over his hips. 'Getting these trousers off is easier said than done when you're standing up,' she murmured.

'Might be easier if we took this to the bed,' he said. The bed that had caused so much angst and yet was just right for the two of them.

She ran her fingers up his chest. 'I'd be happy to take you up against the wall,' she murmured huskily. 'Floor, chair—wherever we might happen to end up. But the bed might be more comfortable. I just want you, Josh.'

'I want you too, Ellie,' he groaned. 'I think you know that.'

She brushed her fingers lightly across the front of his trousers. 'Oh, yes, I can tell.'

He cupped her face in his hands and looked down into her eyes. 'But before we go any further—'

'To the point of no return?'

'There's something I have to tell you; it's important and I—'

'No. We've done more than enough talking.' She silenced him with a kiss. The kiss deepened and became more urgent. *She wanted more than kissing.* All she could think of was making love with Josh. If what he wanted to say was that important he could tell her later.

Josh effortlessly swept her up into his arms and carried her to the bed. He kicked off his shoes and she helped rid him of his trousers and boxers. As she did so, she made admiring comments about what she found beneath them. She had to touch and explore, which made him groan with want and heightened desire for both of them.

In turn, he kissed his way down her stomach, giving her almost unbearable tremors of pleasure and anticipation. He took her lacy thong in his teeth and tugged it over her hips and down her legs, managing a lot of highly arousing kissing of very sensitive places on the way.

She took him by the shoulders. 'Josh. No more. I want you inside me. Now. Please.'

He reached for protection from his wallet and obliged.

'Yes,' she moaned as he pushed inside her body. *Josh.* He felt so hard, so powerful, so *right*. Almost immediately, she shattered into a climax and then another followed when he came.

'Oh, my gosh, what happened there?' she said, flushed and satisfied, with post-orgasmic tremors still rippling deliciously through her. *The best sex of her life.* 'I couldn't wait.'

He pushed her hair away from her face where it was falling out of its pins. 'There's a time for fast and furious and now there's the time for a slow exploration,' he said.

She shimmied her body under him. 'That sounds very good to me. Shall I start by exploring you?'

'Let's explore each other,' he said. 'There's still more to learn about pleasing you.'

He was a fast learner.

Afterwards, she fell asleep in his arms. Some time later they both woke, very early—near dawn, judging from the light in the room—and wordlessly they made love again, as she let her body say what she couldn't say in words.

Josh woke to the morning sun streaming through the French doors. He and Eloise had had more important activities to occupy themselves with the previous night than to draw the curtains. Naked, she lay close to him, one hand resting on his shoulder, a long, slender leg resting across his. The sheets were rumpled across her hips, leaving her beautiful breasts bared. Her hair glinted blue-black in a shaft of sunlight that fell across her face, the same shaft he suspected had woken him.

She looked…different. Then he realised her face was free of cosmetics. He vaguely remembered her getting up at some stage to go and wash her face, saying she never slept in her make-up.

Her skin was ivory pale and smooth with a smattering of light freckles on her cheekbones, her natural lashes dark and luxuriant, her mouth an unadorned pink. Her fingernails painted red were the only artifice, short and neatly shaped. He imagined it wouldn't be so easy to negotiate a sewing machine with long nails. She'd taken off the ruby ring. This Eloise, without her props of attention-getting vintage-style clothes and careful make-up was lovely, a natural beauty. But he liked both looks. He liked Eloise, period.

Aware, perhaps, of his gaze on her, she stirred and opened her lovely blue eyes. She blinked. 'Josh?' Then smiled. '*Josh*,' she said, this time with warmth. She stretched with unconscious grace then rested on her elbow to face him. 'Last night. We broke every rule. And wasn't it wonderful?' A slow, sensual smile spread across her face.

Her hair had tumbled down from its style of the night before, and he pushed it back from her face. 'It was indeed wonderful. *You* were wonderful.' He dropped a kiss on her bare shoulder. He had kissed practically everywhere else on her body last night.

'Thank you. It goes without saying so were you.' She paused. 'It...it wasn't just sex for me.'

'No. Not for me either.'

'I wish—'

'I want—'

They spoke at the same time.

'You say what you were going to say,' she said.

'No, you go first.'

'I was going to say, I wish you didn't live in Boston.'

'And I was going to say, I want to find a way we could continue to see each other after I go back.' He'd been thinking of nothing else since they'd first made love. That, and how he could explain why he hadn't told her about Tori, and that their meeting hadn't been accidental. Fact was, the more he'd got to know her, the harder it had been to tell her because the more there was at risk in terms of him and her.

'You mean long-distance dating? I'm not sure that—'

'We can try and make it work. If we want it enough. And I do, Ellie—'

'I like it when you call me Ellie.'

'I'm glad,' he said. 'But don't change the subject. I want to try to keep something going between us. At least try and see how it pans out.'

She traced a finger down his nose and over his mouth. He caught it with his teeth. 'I like that,' she murmured as she took it away. 'It's not just the long distance. I… I'm frightened of liking you too much.'

'Why is that?'

'The more I like you, the more I open myself to hurt.'

'I wouldn't hurt you.'

'Not intentionally, perhaps.'

'Certainly not intentionally. Have you been hurt before?' He felt a rush of anger at the thought of anyone hurting her.

'Hasn't everyone?' she said.

'That's not what I asked,' he said. He had to know what he was up against.

'I've been hurt. Of course, I've hurt people too. Men I never should have dated.'

He didn't give a flying fig about the men she had hurt. Although maybe he should. She could have the power to hurt him too—there were definite fissures in that shield around his heart, chiselled by each kiss from this wonderful woman. 'I don't care about them. It's you who interests me.'

She sighed. 'I started off a romantic, totally believing in happy-ever-after. My parents had a wonderful marriage—classic love at first sight, totally devoted to each other. I honestly thought it would be as easy as that for me too. Meet Mr Right in a shower of moonbeams, fall in love, glide up that aisle. The realities of teenage dating soon beat that delusion out of me. Me, all starry-eyed; him willing to gabble *I love you* as many times as it took to get what he wanted.'

'That guy was a jerk. Not all boys were like that. Boys get their hearts broken too.'

'Did you?'

'Yes. Probably part of the reason I'm propelled by bitterness and revenge.'

She bit her bottom lip. 'I'm sorry I said that. It was harsh.'

'But true. You were right. Meeting you has made me think about how I'm living my life, that maybe it's not, as you say, so healthy. I need to look forward, not trip myself up by looking backwards for my motivation. But that doesn't explain why you're frightened of liking me too much.'

'When my father died, my mother fell to pieces. An intelligent, capable person like her was utterly lost without him. It took her years to get back on her feet, though she's never remarried. I saw that and it scared me—the power of love, the pain when you lose it for whatever reason.'

'So you anticipate the end before you risk the beginning? I'm sorry. But that was your parents. What about you?'

'The first time I really fell in love was with a guy in Paris. He loved me too. But we couldn't keep it going long-distance. I was heartbroken. Couldn't look at anyone else for a long time.'

Jealousy, irrational but powerful, seared through him. He couldn't bear the thought of her with any other man. It shocked him. He'd only known her a week.

'How old were you?'

'Nineteen.'

'You probably couldn't have afforded to keep it going. That wouldn't be an issue with us.'

'True. But you know it isn't your wealth that interests me?'

'If I thought that for even a second, I wouldn't be here.' He dropped a kiss on her mouth.

'I value my independence and I'm frightened of giving over even part of my life for someone else to control. That last guy…the one I told you about who lied to me about who he really was? He made me distrust my own judgement.'

'Why does it have to be like that? My father had to have everyone under his control. Your parents were of a different generation. So were mine. When I turned eighteen, when she thought I didn't need her any more, my mother went back to my father. Of course, *I* still wasn't welcome at the house.'

'Oh, Josh, no wonder you're bitter.'

'I haven't got a great track record with relationships. As I told you, I've been a lone wolf. "He who travels fastest, travels alone." That kind of thing. But meeting you…meeting you is making me look at things differently. Making me think it could be worth taking a risk.'

'I seem to attract men who want to take charge of me. The last guy was like that too.'

'What foolish men they must be,' he said, smiling. 'If I've ever seen anyone who is her own woman, it's you. It's one of the things I like about you.'

'But would you want to change me?'

'I don't think so. I like you exactly as you are. But how would we know that, if we didn't get to know each other better? It's only been days, though it seems I've known you longer. I haven't had much practice in making compromises, and maybe you've made too many. We won't know unless we try.'

'All I ask is honesty,' she said. 'I can't forgive lies. Oh, I know we've fibbed our hearts out about the engagement, but that's different; that's—'

'A targeted business strategy of purposeful evasion,' he said.

'You remembered?'

'How could I forget?'

'You're laughing at me.'

'I'm not. I think it's brilliant. But there is

something I have to tell you. There's someone back in Boston.'

'A girl?'

'Yes, but it's not what you think. She's a
very good friend and—'

'I don't think I want to hear about it.'

'You should because—'

The phone in the room rang. He looked at
Eloise and she looked back. 'I suppose we'd
better answer it.'

She got out of bed and walked over to the
desk where the handset was. She was completely unselfconsciously naked, and utterly
enticing. He lay back against the pillow and
admired the shapely lines of her beautiful body. That feeling of being on shifting
ground returned. He felt as if he was on the
edge of something new and important and
life-changing. *Because of her.*

She picked up the phone and listened.
'Thank you,' she said and hung up. She turned
to him. 'Breakfast for the house guests is being
served in the conservatory for another hour.
Do you—?'

'I'd rather skip breakfast and have you back
here in bed with me.' Could he ever have
enough of her?

'Other appetites, huh?' she said. 'I couldn't agree with you more.'

She slid back under the covers. 'Thank heaven they gave us this great big bed.'

'Oh, I don't know,' he said, pulling her close to him. 'I think we could happily have found our way around any size bed.'

CHAPTER THIRTEEN

By the time he and Eloise had left Silver Trees, stopped for lunch in Bowral and driven the two hours back to Sydney, it was mid-afternoon when she dropped Josh back to his hotel. He'd arranged to spend a few hours there and then go around to her apartment to take her out to dinner. They planned to talk seriously about how they might be the couple who could actually make long-distance work.

But before he did that, he had to call Tori. He hadn't been honest with her about how he felt about Eloise. But then, he hadn't been honest with himself—fighting the fact he was falling for her. Right from that first meeting in the park.

Tori was pleased to hear from him. He realised how difficult it must be for her not to know what was happening on the other side of the world. But why the hell hadn't she connected with Eloise as soon as he'd told her he was certain they were twins? It would have made it so much more straightforward for him. Now it was complicated. Too complicated.

'How did the wedding go?' Tori asked.

'So you remembered that was yesterday?'

'That you were my twin sister's plus-one at some big society wedding? Well, yeah. That wasn't something I'd easily forget.'

He'd known Tori since he was sixteen, but he wasn't sure how to voice this. 'It was good. Very good. But I haven't been completely honest with you.'

He could sense her frown through the phone. 'What do you mean?'

'About Eloise. And me. Remember you told me not to develop a thing for her? It was already too late. It's more than a thing. I'm in love with her.'

There was an indrawn hiss from Tori. 'Josh. That wasn't meant to happen.'

'I know. But it did.'

'You've fallen in love with a woman who looks just like me? Don't you think that's a little weird?'

'Not weird at all. She's actually nothing like you. I mean that in a good way. You complement each other. You'd see that if you met her. What I'm saying, Tori, is that you have to get in touch with her. I can't keep lying— to her or to you.'

'Are you serious, Josh?'

'Serious about Eloise?' He paused. 'Yeah. I am.'

'I've never heard you say that before. Finally he meets the right woman. And it has to be the twin sister I've never met. In Australia. You should have told me earlier.'

'I wasn't sure. But I've told you now. Call her. Please.'

It was corny, he knew, but Josh arrived at Eloise's apartment building that evening bearing flowers. It wasn't something he remembered ever having done since he'd bought a corsage for his prom date back in high school. The florist in the lobby of the hotel was open and on impulse he bought a huge bunch of voluptuous deep pink roses that he thought she might like. A gesture, perhaps, of how different he intended his life to be now. All part of him embracing 'the kinder side of life'. A life with Eloise in it.

He still firmly believed that her connection with Eloise was Tori's secret to tell, and the truth of their sisterhood should only be revealed twin to twin. And yet there had to be total honesty between him and Eloise for their fledgling—so new the feathers were still damp and crumpled—relationship to have a chance. Tori had had a few hours to call Eloise. He hoped like hell she had. Because he couldn't move forward with Eloise until she knew about Tori. And about the part he'd played in the discovery of the twins. How he'd seen that magazine article and pointed it out to Tori; how he'd offered to help by looking up Eloise while he was in Sydney—and why he'd had to evade the truth.

As he waited for Eloise to buzz him through the security door to the block, he tried to put a name to the way he was feeling. Finally he settled on elation. Elation at the prospect of seeing her again. Of being able to explain what had happened. Elation at the prospect of her becoming someone significant in his life. He hadn't felt like this about a woman for a long time. In fact, he'd never felt like this about a woman because he'd never met a woman like Eloise.

However, the second she opened the door of her apartment to him he knew something was amiss. Her face seemed drained of her usual vivacity, her mouth set in a grim line. She seemed, in a way, diminished. When he lowered his head to kiss her, he really knew something was wrong.

She averted her face, shrugged him away. 'Don't touch me,' she said coldly. She looked at the flowers with an expression he could only describe as scorn.

'What's wrong?' he asked, perplexed. How fleeting had been that feeling of elation. It had come crashing down to smother him.

Eloise stomped away from him into the living room, as if she couldn't bear to even breathe the same air as him, then whirled back to face him. 'I've just spent the last hour on a video chat with Tori. My twin sister Tori. The sister I had no idea I had, but of course you did.' Her cheeks were flushed.

Good. Tori had delivered. But her call didn't seem to have had the effect he'd hoped for.

'She called you.' He put the flowers down on a side table.

'She did. Can you imagine what it was like for me? First to find out I had a twin sister. And second to discover you're a friend of hers and have known about this all the time.

That you've completely misrepresented yourself. And let me…let me get to like you. You
played games with Tori too, with our fake
engagement. I had to sort her out about that.'

'But how—?' What had Tori said?

'Funnily enough, Tori follows @lindythe-
blonde. I told you, millions do. So what does
she see but a post mentioning our engagement? With a photo of us dancing very close
and looking as though we wanted to tear each
other's clothes off on the dance floor.'

'Which we probably did.'

'That's beside the point. For me, *you* are
now beside the point.'

Her words felt like a kick to the gut. There
were no words of his own he could summon
up in reply.

'You'd know better than I do why she
hadn't contacted me earlier, but apparently
seeing us "engaged" put a bomb up her. I suspect she wasn't at all happy about it.'

'No,' he said. He had omitted to tell Tori
about the fake engagement. He should have.
She didn't know it was fake. It hadn't seemed
important. Not as important as Tori contact-
ing Eloise and telling her the truth. But it
must have been a shock. And to see him look-

ing so intimate with Eloise when she'd only just found out they were together.

Tori would be furious he hadn't told her he was engaged. Even though he actually wasn't. And that was on top of him not telling her about his feelings for Eloise until today. But his attraction to Eloise had been a force of its own. What had happened with Eloise had developed completely independently of Tori. It had been too private, too personal to share with anyone. It had overridden even his loyalty to his friend. Quite frankly, his intimate time with Eloise was none of Tori's business. Being lovers, a couple, meant sharing their own private, special world with no one else but each other. He'd found that magical world with Eloise, and now he could see it slipping away.

'Tori contacted me over social media, outlining the story of the twins adopted separately when they were two years old, telling me she believed I was her sister.'

He took a step towards her, wanting to comfort her. 'That must have been a shock.'

She took a step back, pointedly rejecting him. 'You could say that. It brought back in its entirety the shock of finding I'd been adopted. Tori had only just discovered that

Baby One—me—had been adopted to a Boston couple, Dr Debra Evans and Dr Adam Evans—my parents, of course. Tori was Baby Two, adopted to Marissa Preston and Tom Preston, also of Boston.'

'She'd been waiting for that information as confirmation.' Josh felt as if he was pushing his way through thick sand, caught in a quagmire of deception that hadn't been entirely of his own making.

'And you knew that. *You knew.*' She spat the accusation.

'Yes,' was all he could manage to choke out, his mind racing to see how—if—he could salvage something from this.

'She sent me a photo of her. It was like looking at me with short hair. A…a different version of me. I nearly hyperventilated. You see stories in the media about this kind of thing. You don't expect in a million years that you could find yourself in the story.'

'I'm sorry.' He'd made a few abortive attempts to tell her something of the story, but had still not been sure how much had been his to tell.

He could have prepared her for this. Or could he have? Not without revealing she might have a twin sister. He was stymied whichever path he took. But at least Eloise was telling him what had happened and hadn't booted him straight out of the door. Although that might be because he was the only other person she knew who also knew Tori and she needed to talk about her.

Eloise raked her fingers through her hair. 'Tori asked could we video chat? Before I considered that option, I called my mother. She was as shocked as I was—she'd had no idea there were two babies; neither apparently did Tori's adoptive mother. I suspect both the mothers would have had a moment, even for a split second, of wondering what it would have been like if they'd been given the other baby.'

'Why didn't you call me?'

'I had no idea there was a connection to you at that stage. It was something so intensely personal I had to do it for myself. *A sister.* Then tell you about it afterwards.'

'So what happened on the call?'

Tori was obviously so cranky with him about leaving her out of the engagement news, she hadn't presented him in a favourable light. He wished he'd known that before he'd come over here with his goofy bunch of roses. Because he knew where this was head-

ing. Had known when Eloise had so pointedly averted her face from his kiss. But he
wouldn't give up without a fight. He was in
love with her.

'I couldn't believe it,' she said, the wonder
and shock still in her voice. 'At first we just
stared at each other for what seemed a long
time without saying a word. I saw *myself* on
the screen. I wanted to put out my hand to
touch her. To see if she was real. It was seriously like looking in the mirror. We're the
same, yet I think we're very different people.
She dresses in a rock chick kind of style. But
then, you know that, don't you? You've been
friends since high school. Only friends, she
reassured me. Strictly platonic.'

'I think of her like a sister; her family
were good to me,' he said. 'Remember I told
you how my mother and I went to live with
my aunt in the North End? I met Tori at my
new school. She took the new kid under her
wing.'

'Yeah. She said that.' Her tone was frigid.
As if his role in this was irrelevant. As if he
was no longer relevant to her.

'She has two brothers. Great guys. Did she
tell you that?'

'She did. Our lives growing up were very

different. But it seems we both had good adoptive parents.'

'So did you like each other? I was sure you would.'

Her face softened. But for Tori, not for him.

'Immediately we clicked. Certain things fell into place. We were together until we were two years old, so must have buried memories of each other. We both felt something was missing in our lives. Turned out I was her imaginary friend. She was the picture I drew for my mother as the sister I wanted. There were other weird things. We both broke our left arms when we were ten. Had our appendix out at the same time. Both creative and into art and design. Both work with rescue dogs. And seriously weird that we each have wedding-related businesses. Dresses for me, cakes for her.'

'Not weird but a twin thing, I guess.' Maybe a bit weird considering the sisters hadn't seen each other for twenty-six years. 'I'm so happy for you both—it's an amazing thing to have found a sister.' He didn't want to point out that he was the one who had actually found her. It would not be appreciated, he was certain of that.

'It got very emotional; we were both crying

by the end. Of course we'll get DNA tested. Did you know identical twins share almost one hundred per cent the same DNA? But we don't need a test to know we're sisters. And there was another thing. I talked to her on my laptop in my bedroom. She noticed on the shelf behind me a small, pink stuffed rabbit. I've had it ever since I can remember. Tori left the camera for a minute and came back with an identical one in her hand. A bit more battered than mine, as she grew up with two brothers, but she'd been told it was from her birth mother. I guess mine was from my birth mother too. But of course I'd never been told that. Maybe my parents didn't know its significance.'

Josh ached to take her into his arms and comfort her. Finding out about Tori was obviously a positive thing for her, but a deeply emotional one. One she would need quite some getting used to. He wanted to hug her and tell her everything he knew about Tori and what a wonderful person her newly found sister was. But she'd folded her arms across her chest and the emanations coming from her were distinctly hostile.

'I won't offer you a drink or a snack or even a seat,' she said. 'Because you won't be staying. I can't believe I was fooled by you when I so wanted to believe in you.'

'But you can still believe in me, Ellie.'

Her bottom lip stuck out, just like Tori's did when she was angry. They were sisters all right. 'Don't call me Ellie.'

Another kick to the gut.

'How can you honestly think I could believe anything you say? Tori told me everything. How you discovered a picture of me in a magazine and pointed out the resemblance. How you volunteered to look me up when you were here to report back to Tori in Boston.'

'I had no doubt, that first day in the park, that you were twins.'

'And you kept that to yourself. Even…even when we became lovers. How could you have done that?'

'Out of loyalty to Tori. It was her right to tell you. Wouldn't you do the same for a friend? Wouldn't you want to help if it was, say, Vinh? If you had a friend, a good friend who had taken you into her family when your own family had dumped you. A friend who had always felt something—someone—was missing in her life. Wouldn't you help her find her look-alike who just might be her identical twin?'

'I wouldn't completely misrepresent myself like you did.'

'Tori made me promise not to say anything to you. I respected that. It was her secret, her story. Your story and your sister's story. It wasn't mine to tell.'

'But you let things get so far between us.'

'That's where Tori doesn't know the full story. I said I'd try to find you and get a close look at you to check you really were her double as you appeared to be. Photos can lie. But I didn't count on being attracted to you. On not being able to stop thinking about you. That's why I flew back up from Melbourne—just so I could see you again.'

'But you said—'

'I know. I made new business appointments in Sydney to justify the trip, unable at that stage to admit to myself it was really all about you. That was real. What happened last night was real. Those…those feelings were real.'

Slowly she shook her head. 'It doesn't change anything, Josh. I could never trust another word you said. Everything you said to me last night and this morning, I wanted to believe it. And you know what? It makes me distrust Tori too.'

'You can trust her. Tori had no idea about

our fake engagement or what happened between us at Silver Trees.'

'Don't talk about what happened between us. Don't remind me that I trusted you, believed in you. Now I… I never want to see you again, Josh.'

'Please, Eloise, don't say that. I'm sorry about how I handled this. Above all, I didn't want to hurt you. Ever.' He wasn't one to beg and plead, but he also didn't want to let go what he'd found with her without a fight.

'Hurt? Why would I be hurt? It was, after all, only one night. I… I hadn't had time to get attached.'

One night had been enough for him to change his entire way of thinking. 'We talked about making it more than one night.'

'That was before I discovered how you'd lied to me.'

She was hurting, even if she was denying it. He knew her well enough to know that. And that pain had been inflicted by him. He'd tried to do the right thing by Tori and by Eloise too. Reuniting these two sisters could be a wonderful thing for them. The imaginary friend and the girl in the drawing. Now they were both angry with him. A united force.

'Can't we try and start again, Eloise? Now that you know the truth about Tori.'

'No,' she said flatly.

'Perhaps we could meet tomorrow and talk this through?'

'There is absolutely no point. Unless you have further business in Sydney, I suggest you fly back home to Boston.'

'Did last night mean anything to you?' he challenged. It sure as hell had meant something to him.

She raised her chin. 'It was great sex,' she said.

'It was that,' he agreed. Their lovemaking had been so awesome because emotions had been at play that neither of them had been prepared to admit to. Until they'd let down their guards in the morning. *This morning.* It seemed an age ago now. Her barriers were right back up again.

'But that's all,' she said, making absolutely sure he got the message.

It had been so much more than sex for him. But he had no right to argue the point. He had to disengage from her. This aftermath of relationships gone wrong was one of the main reasons he had avoided them for so long.

'The only thing I ask, is if we can keep up

the pretence of the engagement for a while longer,' she said. 'If it gets out now that we're frauds, it will do more harm than good and I'll be a laughing stock.'

'Sure,' he said. 'We'll stick to the timeline. Give it a few months to peter out. You can tell people we're in touch. Fabricate a few phone calls. Whatever you need to do. I'll be in Boston, right out of your way. If someone should happen to ask, I'll give them the same story. Just text me when you decide it's gone on long enough, so we keep our stories straight about ending it. I have no intention of returning to Sydney.' He'd been planning to buy a house here to make it easy to see her.

He was hurt. But he'd had plenty of experience of hiding his hurts. That old shield around his heart would still do its work, and the cracks would eventually mend. He'd stay clear of the Tori-Eloise reunion. He'd done his best to bring them together. Time to bow right out.

'Let me know if you change your mind about meeting,' he said.

Her silence told him she wasn't going to change her mind.

'I'll fly out tomorrow.'

'Good,' she said.

There was nothing good about it, not as far as he was concerned anyway.

'Don't take what happened between us out on Tori,' he said. 'You'll like having her as a sister.'

Wordlessly, she nodded.

'Goodbye, Eloise.'

He turned on his heel and walked out, not looking behind him.

Eloise was left staring after Josh. She had to hold on to the back of a chair for support, take deep breaths to steady herself. How had this wonderful new phase of her life suddenly gone so horribly, horribly wrong?

She'd gained a sister. A twin. *A miracle.* But she'd lost a man she'd thought she could fall in love with. A man she'd started to spin dreams around.

She breathed in the lingering scent of him, mingling with the rich sweetness of those magnificent roses. How did he know they were her favourites?

The same way he knew how to please her in bed, how to make her laugh, how to make her think she was with the most wonderful man on earth. And she'd believed in him.

Only to have that belief thrown back at her by the discovery of his deceit.

She'd had a lucky escape. More time spent with him and she would have been back in that sticky, sweet trap of infatuation. She'd made the same old mistakes, thrown away all her hard-won caution. All for a few exciting kisses, a thrilling time in bed.

Deep down, she knew it had been more than that. There had been an undeniable connection between her and Josh, something so compelling it had overridden caution and common sense. That was what had made it so agonising to find out the truth about him. That he was there in the park that day had been no accident. He'd been there specifically to watch out for her. Mara, the waitress, had recognised him because he'd been sitting at her café hoping to catch sight of her to report back to Tori. What else didn't she know about him? She'd thought she knew enough to trust him.

Eloise knew she couldn't stay here by herself. She'd go crazy with regrets and self-recriminations and a chorus of *what ifs* hammering into her brain. Home. She'd go home to her mother, who'd said for her the discovery of her twin was almost like finding another daughter. She would want to talk about Tori. She'd pick up Daisy, the little dog whose instincts she'd trusted over her own. Which was a kind of crazy all by itself.

CHAPTER FOURTEEN

Three weeks later

THE LAST TIME Eloise had flown into Boston's Logan Airport she'd been fifteen years old and accompanied by her mother and father, arriving from Sydney for their annual trip to her father's hometown. Her grandparents— her father's parents—had been waiting for them when they'd come out of Security. Family. That was what it had been all about then. Her memories were bittersweet: her father had died not long after and she hadn't seen her grandparents since. She was tempted to contact them while she was here—maybe they'd mellowed—but wasn't sure she could handle their rejection.

Today she'd flown in from New York and she was also being greeted by family. Her twin sister, Tori. Her blood family. Since the first day they'd connected online they'd chatted most days, even if only for minutes at a time. The need to see each other face to face had become overwhelming. And the opportunity to meet came sooner rather than later. She could hardly wait to hug the sister she hadn't seen since she was two years old.

She'd be meeting Tori's parents and brothers too, which was exciting. As for Josh... Tori knew to keep his name right off the reception committee. During their online chats, Eloise had specifically asked her new-found sister not to talk about Josh. How could she forget him any other way?

Eloise had spent the last week in New York City. Roxee's actress friend's wedding had turned into a mega celebration with twelve bridesmaids and three changes of gown for the bride. It was a job that had required Eloise's hands-on presence. The American side of the business was burgeoning and getting more and more time-consuming. Not just for the actual design and production of the garments but also the tariffs and taxes on importing Australian-made products into the United States and the consequent paperwork. Then there were the celebrities impatient at being put on an ever-growing waiting list.

It was getting to the stage that the balance

was starting to tip between her Australian clients and her clients in the USA. She had to be careful not to overstretch herself—that could be the death of creativity, and she'd seen it too many times when designer friends had started their own labels and ended up bankrupt.

She might have to establish an atelier in New York, perhaps put Vinh in charge. But the fact was it was her name on the label. And it was Eloise Evans those demanding new clients wanted to see, certainly in the first instance.

She should be deliriously happy about her business's rapid expansion. Trouble was, she couldn't take much joy in it.

'You've had too many emotional ups and downs,' her mother had said soothingly. Her mum knew about Josh, as Eloise had sobbed out her distress on her shoulder.

'There are plenty of other fish in the sea,' her mother's advice had been. That was always her relationship advice. She didn't think any of Eloise's boyfriends had been worthy of her daughter. This time, Eloise suspected she was secretly glad things hadn't worked out with Josh. She didn't want to lose her only child to Boston.

Her mother had joined in some of the video

chats with Tori. 'We've found each other, but we've also each found a new family,' Tori had said several times in delight.

So the deeply hidden gap in Eloise's life caused by her long-lost sister had been filled. Sadly there was now another painful gap: Josh. True to their agreement, they hadn't contacted each other. For her own well-being, she needed to forget he'd ever been in her life. So why did she miss him so much? She couldn't go to her favourite café in the park, the restaurant where they'd had their first date, even Mara's café near her work. So many memories for such a short time together. And that was apart from the dreams that haunted her sleep and had her waking to tears when she realised he wasn't there. Poor Daisy had had her fur wetted with tears, but the little dog had only given her comfort. Eloise didn't know how she would bear to give this dog away. She might have to admit to being a foster fail and keep her.

She cleared Security and watched out for...well, someone who looked like herself. And there she was: black hair like hers but chopped short and spiky, wearing urban chic black jeans and boots. And a huge smile.

Her sister. *The sister Josh had found for*

her. She hadn't appreciated just what he'd done and the conflicting loyalties he'd had to struggle with, the integrity with which he had treated both her and Tori. Only now, meeting her twin and realising the incredible odds against having found her, did she realise just how grateful she should have been to Josh. Instead she had pushed him away. And wounded herself in the process. But she couldn't think about that now. She was in Boston. She would have to swallow her pride and seek him out. Grovel a little— okay, grovel a lot. And hope he would give her the second chance she'd refused to give him. Even if only to be friends as they had Tori in common.

She and Tori hugged, then drew back to look at each other and exclaim at their resemblance and then hugged again. Tears flowed too, happy and emotional.

'I didn't think we'd look quite so alike,' Tori said. 'It's uncanny. Even the video chat didn't give the complete story. Our height, the way we move, our expressions.'

'The full dimension. If we'd grown up together, can you imagine the fun we would have had swapping places and tricking people?' Eloise said.

'Oh, yes!' said Tori, laughing. Her laugh was like an echo of Eloise's own. 'We would have been menaces.'

'We were cheated of that childhood,' Eloise said slowly. 'I wonder why?'

'I couldn't find out why the adoption agency split us up.'

'I guess they had their reasons. But it turned out well for both of us, didn't it?' Eloise said. She couldn't stop smiling.

'We were both so blessed with our adoptive families,' said Tori.

'We were indeed. And now we've found each other.'

'With no intention of ever losing one another again.'

Arms around each other, they walked towards the area where Tori must have parked her car. A few people did a double take when they saw them together and Eloise and her sister laughed. 'There might be possibilities for us to be menaces still,' Eloise said. They both giggled. In harmony.

When they'd stopped laughing, Tori spoke. 'There's someone I want you to meet. A friend of mine.'

'A bride in need of a dress?'

'No, a guy friend.'

Eloise stopped her with a hand on her arm. 'Please, Tori, that's sweet of you, but I really don't want to be set up with anyone. Seriously. I'm happy on my own. I don't have time to date or the inclination.' Or the heart. No one could compare to Josh.

'This guy's a really good friend and...'

And then Eloise saw him. Her heart jolted. *Josh*.

He saw her at the same time and he stared, momentarily transfixed. Then he strode towards them. 'Tori, what the hell—?'

All Eloise's denials of her feelings for him, all the anger she'd tried to build up for him deceiving her, were lost in a rush of sheer joy. *Josh*. Josh, even more handsome than she remembered him in a dark, charcoal business suit.

Frowning, he looked to her then to Tori and back to her. He'd been set up. He obviously had no idea why he was here. A well-meaning yet clumsy attempt by her sister to force them together? She wanted to cringe with the humiliation of it. Then she looked at Josh, really looked at him. And saw the same emotions she was trying to control herself reflected in his hazel eyes. And, strangely, he didn't look as if he wanted to be anywhere but here.

'This is my friend Josh Taylor,' said Tori, as if Eloise had never met the man before. Or made love with him, or laughed with him, or teased him as she'd pinned him into a tuxedo.

Tori continued. 'Josh is an excellent friend. The absolute best. He actually found you for me, my long-lost twin. He saw you in a magazine and realised we must be related. Although I think there's actually more to it than that. Josh saw something in that Australian fashion designer that absolutely fascinated him. What he didn't expect was that when he actually met her—at my request—he'd be so madly attracted to her he'd go right off plan in his pursuit of her. Until it wasn't as much about Josh finding my twin for me but about Josh finding the ideal woman for him.'

Eloise swallowed hard against a sudden lump in her throat. She looked up at Josh. 'Is that what happened?' she asked him.

The busy airport around her faded away. Even Tori disappeared. It was just him and her and that connection that had been there from the get go, which she'd done her best to sever with her own insecurities and fears.

'Sounds accurate,' he said, his gaze on her face as if he'd been starved of the sight of her for too long. Something that had been shrivelled and frozen deep inside her since she'd watched him walk out of her apartment started to warm and thaw. *Her heart.*

'Then Josh somehow lost his ideal woman and I don't really know why.' Tori turned to Josh. 'But I think he could tell you that better than I could.' She looked at her watch in an exaggerated manner. 'Heck, I've got to go and see a lady about a cake. Josh, could you get Eloise to the trattoria for me? No rush. In your own time. You okay with that, Eloise? We can catch up later.'

Eloise nodded. Bemused, she watched her sister stride away. 'Is she always like that?'

'She's her own woman. Like you. And she's got it into her head it's her fault that I lost you. Whereas I did a perfectly good job of doing that on my own.'

'You didn't lose me, Josh. I misjudged you. Behaved stupidly. And didn't trust in what we had together.'

'I didn't fully recognise what we'd found. Because I'd never felt it before. Too used to being fuelled by bitterness and revenge I guess.'

She smiled at that. 'I've done pretty well on the bitterness front myself,' she said. 'There I was, lecturing you about the kind side of life, and I was so mean to you.'

Over and over again she'd gone over that final confrontation in her living room, scented with his beautiful roses. 'I cannot believe I told you that you were "beside the point".' She shuddered. 'I'm surprised you're even talking to me.'

'It wounded me, I won't deny it. But you were in shock. I've thought about it a lot. That day. A call from a sister you didn't know existed. Your world knocked off its axis. I wouldn't—I don't—blame you for anything you said. I should have handled it better. Stuck around in Sydney, for one thing. So I'd be there if you needed me. To talk you through things. Helped you understand what had happened.'

'But I pushed you away.'

'I shouldn't have gone. I've been miserable without you.'

She looked up at him. 'I've been miserable without you too. Utterly miserable. Every minute of every day. I think the word might be heartbroken. And I'm so grateful to Tori for engineering this meeting.'

'She didn't need to trick me into seeing you. I've got a ticket to fly out to Sydney tomorrow.'

'But you said you'd never visit Sydney again.'

'I said a lot of things I didn't mean. And left unsaid too many others.'

'Like what, Josh?' She had a few words left unsaid of her own. She held her breath for his answer.

He cupped her face in his hands and looked deeply into her eyes. 'That I love you, Ellie.'

She let out her breath on a sigh of happiness. 'Funnily enough, those are the exact same words I left unsaid. I love you too, Josh. So much. I feared I was falling in love with you at Silver Trees, but I realise I was already head over heels.'

'You've got nothing to fear now, darling Ellie.'

At last he took her in his arms and his kiss was long and tender, at the same time hinting at the passion she knew could ignite so quickly. But, while they were in a busy arrivals hall, where no one would look askance at a couple kissing, she'd rather take the kiss further, which meant going somewhere more appropriate. Like his apartment. She would suggest they detour there on the way to Tori's family trattoria, where a welcome lunch was planned for her.

'Another thing, Josh.'

'Yes?'

'Did you enjoy being my fake fiancé?'

'Very much so. I've never enjoyed myself as much as at the wedding at Silver Trees.'

She took a deep breath. 'Would you consider being my fiancé for real?'

He didn't look the slightest bit perturbed by her proposal. 'On one condition,' he said. 'Two, in fact.'

'What would they be?'

'One that we get our own engagement ring. A ring that's significant just to us that we choose together. You can wear your grandma's ruby on your other hand if you like.'

'Yes. I'd like that. And the other condition?'

'That you be my real-life wife as soon as we can possibly get married. I don't want to wait.'

Joy bubbled through her. 'Yes to that too. I can't think of anything I'd like better. If anyone can organise a wedding in a hurry, it's me. I've got all the contacts.'

'We've wasted enough time apart. Let's get on with our lives together, starting from now.' And he kissed her again.

CHAPTER FIFTEEN

Another three weeks later

ELOISE'S WEDDING DAY. Her twin sister, Tori, and her best friend, Vinh, as her bridesmaids. Josh waiting for her at the altar of the beautiful old sandstone church near Bowral with Tori's two brothers, Ty and Tate, beside him. Eloise thought it couldn't be more perfect. Except her father wasn't there. But her mother was here in the vestibule of the church with her, ready to walk her down the aisle, and she was so grateful for that.

Vinh fussed around her, smoothing and tucking her gown into place. Vinh had helped her design it. Made in heavy white silk, with a full skirt, a stand-up neckline and long, heavy lace sleeves, it gave a nod to her beloved nineteen-fifties vintage style, but was very much a contemporary masterpiece from Eloise Evans Atelier. There was, of course, a detachable train, glistening with crystals, harking back to her mermaid days.

'I've never seen a more beautiful wedding dress,' Tori said wistfully. 'If I ever meet a guy I want to marry, can you make me one just like it, please?'

'I'll make you whatever dress you'd like,' Eloise said.

She and Tori had further bonded through tales of their lacklustre love lives. Pre-Josh, of course, for her. Tori had a huge crush on one of the customers of her bakery, a wealthy architect, but had never done anything about it.

'As alike this one as you can make it, please,' Tori said. 'It's my dream dress.'

'Mine too,' said Eloise, giving her sister a quick at-arm's-length hug so as not to disturb her dress and veil.

The organ started to play the wedding march. Her mother took her arm. 'Time to walk up that aisle, sweetie,' she said. 'There's a good man waiting for you at the altar.' Josh had won her mother over completely and reassured her she would always be welcome to visit, and that they would be in Sydney often.

'I know,' Eloise said simply.

Tori walked first, then Vinh, and finally Eloise started her journey up the aisle of the church full of family and friends towards the man she adored. She realised it was happening just as she'd hoped it would all those years ago before she'd let herself get cynical. Love at first sight. Moonbeams and roses. And a walk up the aisle to where Mr Perfect was waiting for her. All set for the happy-ever-after that awaited them.

So many times at so many weddings, she'd watched for the groom to catch his first sight of his bride. Now she was waiting to see when Josh first saw her. He did not disappoint. Love and wonder and awe shone from his eyes. Her heart turned over and she hoped he saw love and trust and joy in hers as she held his gaze. Her husband-to-be.

Josh placed the platinum wedding band on the third finger of Eloise's left hand above her exquisite diamond ring as he promised to love, honour and cherish her for as long as they both did live. *His wife*. Then he smiled at her as she placed the matching wide band on his ring finger. In fact, he couldn't stop smiling. 'I love you,' she whispered. When the priest pronounced them man and wife, he thought his heart would burst with pride and love.

This was what a kinder life was about.

Love. Friendship. Family. Not that he would stop making millions. It was in his nature to strive and succeed, be ruthless when he needed to be. But everything he did would be for Eloise and the children they hoped to have. Not for an ill-placed, unhealthy revenge.

When the priest said he could kiss the bride, he didn't want to stop.

Eloise had followed the newer custom of changing into another less formal white gown for the reception, which was being held at Silver Trees, thanks to the generosity of Becca and Simon. It was easy for her to have two dresses—after all, she owned two branches of her atelier. Or she would soon when Eloise Evans Atelier, Boston, opened in the exclusive shopping area on Newbury Street.

The timing had been perfect. She'd taken Vinh into partnership with her for the Double Bay branch, while she would work between Sydney and Boston. She and Josh would live in his Seaport apartment while they looked for a house near the North End. She'd be near her twin too.

There was another reason she had chosen to wear a second dress. Her bridal gown was now carefully wrapped in acid-free tissue paper and boxed for Tori to take home with her to Boston. She sought her out, to tell her it was waiting for her in her room.

'It's a good luck wedding dress, I just know it,' Eloise said. 'We're the same size. Take it home with you. I had to learn to trust and open my heart to love. Go after your dream man, the architect. What's his name again?'

'Clay Ramos. But Ellie, I'm not sure—'

'Who knows what might happen? And the dress will be ready for you if it does.'

She hugged her twin, already so loved. She might not see her again until she got back to Boston when she and Josh returned from their honeymoon on a luxury tropical island in far north Queensland.

Josh was over near the table where their magnificent wedding cake—whipped up by Tori—was displayed. He'd been talking to his Melbourne friends and fellow billionaires, Courtney and Shawn. Now he was chatting with his mother, who had defied her husband to travel to Australia to attend her younger son's wedding. His Aunt Lily was here some-where too.

'You know, I was just telling Mom that the only person—well, not a person—we love who's missing from our wedding celebration is Daisy the dog.'

'Funny you should say that,' Eloise said. 'My mother has darling Daisy in her room, with Becca's permission, of course. I thought I'd surprise you by having her at the church but she's still too nervous around a crowd.'

Her move to Boston had made it problematic to adopt Daisy. But her mother had fallen in love with the little dog and decided to adopt her instead, which was nearly as good.

'So Daisy is the dog who introduced you?' Josh's mother asked. Eloise had liked her immediately and looked forward to having her at their home in Boston.

'In a manner of speaking, yes. She will still be part of our lives when we spend time in Sydney. And we can say goodbye to her before we leave.' Tori had already lined her up as a foster carer for a dog rescue organisation in Boston.

'Sounds like the perfect wedding all round,' said Josh. 'Here, where it all started for us.'

'It's the start of our perfect life together as husband and wife,' she said, lifting her face for his kiss.

* * * * *

Look out for the next story in the
How to Make a Wedding duet

From Tropical Fling to Forever
by Nina Singh

Coming soon!

And if you enjoyed this story,
check out these other great reads from
Kandy Shepherd

Their Royal Baby Gift
One Night with Her Millionaire Boss
Falling for the Secret Princess